SHERIFF SLOCUM

BERKLEY BOOKS, NEW YORK

SHERIFF SLOCUM

A Berkley Book / published by arrangement with the author

PRINTING HISTORY
Berkley edition / February 1993

ISBN: 0-425-13624-8

A BERKLEY BOOK ® ™ 757,375
Berkley Books are published by The Berkley Publishing Group.
200 Madison Avenue, New York, New York 10016.
The name "BERKLEY" and "B" logo
are trademarks belonging to Berkley Publishing Corporation.

PRINTED IN THE UNITED STATES OF AMERICA

10 9 8 7 6 5 4 3 2 1

SHERIFF SLOCUM

1

John Slocum finished his hand-rolled cigarette and stubbed out the butt, making sure there was no trace of it left in the rocky soil. Other than this unnecessary caution, he appeared at ease. The two men with him paced like caged animals, checking their side arms every few seconds until Slocum wanted to tell them that the cylinders would never hold more than six rounds.

He leaned back, tipping his dusty, broad-brimmed hat down to shade his green eyes. He watched the pair more carefully. Something was up, and he didn't know what it might be.

The stagecoach robbery shouldn't have gotten them riled like this. Dunphy was an old hand at being a highwayman. And Slocum didn't know much about Barstow's background, but he had the hard look of a man willing to take a life if crossed. That didn't bother Slocum unduly. What did was the way the pair kept glancing in his direction, as if they shared a guilty secret.

"Coach will be along in a spell," Dunphy said, stating the obvious. There wasn't any reason in hell for them to be burning under the noonday sun unless they had important business. Barstow claimed there was a gold shipment on the stagecoach, and from all Slocum had heard, the man was right. A few ounces of gold dust riding in his saddlebags would take him a fair distance west. Right about now,

1

getting out of here was all Slocum wanted.

"Any minute," Slocum allowed, wondering if he ought to bag the robbery. He had stuck up trains and stagecoaches before with nervous men, and he always found himself having to watch his back as much—maybe more—than did the guards trusted with protecting their cargo. Slocum wasn't sure that buck fever was the problem this time.

If he got bushwhacked, it might be from intent rather than nerves.

"There, there it is," said Barstow, straining to see the tiny dust cloud building on the horizon. "It'll be along in ten minutes."

"Less," Slocum said. "I timed it, remember?" He pulled out his brother Robert's watch, flipped open the gold case, and watched the minute hand move slowly. The stage was only five minutes distant. Slocum had scouted the driver's habits carefully, and he always put the whip to the team about now to get them up a long incline. By the time they reached the spot at the foot of the huge broken boulder where the trio of bandits waited, the horses would be lathered and unable to put on a burst of speed to escape.

"Get ready," Barstow said, his nerves showing even more by the way he fingered the butt of his six-shooter. Slocum slipped the watch into his vest pocket and pulled up his blue-and-white bandanna to cover his face. He heaved to his feet and went to his horse, looking now and again over his shoulder. He didn't think either of the men would backshoot him, but they were acting funny. Slocum had stayed alive this long trying to out-figure the other guy.

"Let's get rich," Dunphy said, adjusting his red-checked bandanna. He put spurs to his horse's sides. The animal almost bolted at the sudden request for speed. Slocum took this as another indication of how nervous the other two were. The horse would have thrown Dunphy and damned near killed him if it had broken into a gallop.

Slocum slipped his ebony-handled Navy Colt from his cross-draw holster and cocked it. He didn't think there would be any gunplay. This was going to be a clean robbery unless somebody in the stage got a sudden case of courage.

They made their way down a narrow path through the rocky terrain and came out at just the right time. The team strained to pull the heavy Concord coach up the slope. The driver had exhausted the animals, just as Slocum had predicted.

"Stand and deliver!" bellowed Barstow. The man aimed his six-gun square at the driver. Dunphy covered the shotgun guard, who had been dozing and hadn't seen them in the road. The man came awake with a jerk, started to level his scattergun, and then thought better of it. He dropped it into the driver's box at his feet.

"The strongbox. Toss it down," ordered Barstow. Slocum rode around and peered inside the coach, thinking a few dollars might be had from the passengers. He went cold inside when he saw that the stagecoach was empty. Something was wrong—very wrong. This route always had passengers on their way to San Antonio or Austin.

"Get moving," Slocum called out. "This is a trap!"

Dunphy heaved the strongbox up behind his saddle, then swung back up just as a bullet whizzed past Slocum's ear. He ducked low and looked over his shoulder. Two men with rifles were sniping at him. He saw the bright Texas sun glinting off their badges. They had ridden into an ambush with their eyes wide open.

Slocum started to warn Dunphy and Barstow of the newcomers, then saw that they had simply vanished. The lawmen's rifles were all trained on him. Hot lead sang past his left ear, taking just a nick out of it. A tiny trickle of warm blood ran from the wound, down his neck, and under his collar. Slocum knew it was time to make for the high country.

The driver was fumbling for a hogleg and the shotgun guard had his weapon up and was swinging it around wildly. Slocum wasn't too worried about either of the men on the stagecoach. The thunder of hooves from down the road worried him more. There was an entire damned posse after him.

Using his knees, he turned his horse and got the gelding trotting through the rain of bullets while he drew his Winchester. He levered in a round and let fly at the stagecoach's team. The bullet spooked one of the horses, and that was all Slocum could have hoped for. The driver had to fight to keep his team from running away with him, the shotgun wielding guard was thrown off balance, and the stage blocked the road. This wasn't much of a break, but Slocum used it to the fullest.

"There he goes. Get 'im, Sheriff. Get the son of a bitch. He stole the strongbox!"

Slocum bent low, his head beside his horse's neck. Let the driver yell all he wanted. Slocum could use the extra confusion to mask his getaway, such as it was. He galloped along the road for a half mile, then slowed to keep from tiring the horse too much. Slocum turned the horse off the road and into rocky ground. The going was harder, but tracking would be almost impossible.

What had happened to Dunphy and Barstow? The two had been running before the first shot. A gut-level feeling of betrayal turned inside Slocum like a knife. They took quite a chance if they thought the law was following the coach. But they took very little chance if they knew of the trap and had prepared for it without telling Slocum. They might have some hidden spot to go to ground, letting Slocum lead the posse away from them like some Judas goat. Slocum's fingers danced on the butt of his Colt as he rode along and worked through the possibilities of the pair's treachery. There couldn't be much in the strongbox, but split two ways was better than divvying it up into thirds.

Slocum might be wrong about them, but he didn't think so. He hadn't seen any trace of them as he fled. Not being far behind, he would have detected some spoor. This reinforced his belief that they had a hidey hole and were waiting for the sheriff to catch Slocum. One thief was better than none. When the heat was off, they'd ride on out, pleased as punch with themselves. And richer by the amount of Slocum's share.

"Did they tell the sheriff about the robbery beforehand, or did they just know it was a setup?" Slocum asked his gelding. He patted the horse on the neck to let him know how much he was appreciated. Without the burst of speed and sure-footedness across the rocks he might not have gotten away.

He tried to remember what this section of Texas was like. Rocky desert. Not much water, save for the Rio Grande flowing a few miles off to the west. Or was it to the southwest? Slocum had gotten turned around and needed a map to find the river and the sanctuary it offered. Getting to Mexico was about the smartest trail he could ride right now. It galled him to let his two former partners waltz off scot-free with the money from the robbery, but keeping his own neck from being stretched by a noose was a more immediate concern.

Safety now, revenge later. Slocum didn't doubt that Dunphy and Barstow would get drunk in some saloon and brag about their double dealing. They'd leave a trail a blind man could follow. And Slocum was anything but blind.

He rode steadily the rest of the afternoon, tracing out a zigzag trail, in case the law was still after him. Now and again, he'd find a rise and watch the horizon behind him for any sign of pursuit. The wind had kicked up and swirling dust had obscured his vision for most of the day. This had its good points, along with the bad. Grit worked its way into his mouth and made him want to spit constantly. The obscuring blankets of West Texas dust made tracking him even harder, though, and that was worth a bucket of spit.

A quick meal in late afternoon kept him from riding in the hottest part of the day, but Slocum began to worry about his horse. The gelding was tiring quickly and needed water.

"We'll get into Mexico, and you'll have all the water you want. And grain. You deserve it," he said, a hand on the horse's hindquarters. Slocum fastened his saddlebags and turned, startled by a sudden flash in the afternoon sunlight. He squinted hard, not sure if he had seen the glimmer.

It came again. The flare of sun on a badge. Slocum had seen it too many times not to recognize it instantly.

"They must be half Apache to track us this far," Slocum said to his horse, swinging into the saddle. The horse reluctantly started off at a trot. Slocum kept looking over his shoulder, wondering if he was only imagining that the posse had caught up with him. Then he heard horses— near. Too near.

Cursing, he urged his horse to greater speed. How the damned lawmen had found him in this desolate, dust devil racked desert land he didn't know. It was enough that they had. He might have gotten careless somehow, though he doubted it. However they had tracked him, he couldn't blame this bit of bad luck on either Dunphy or Barstow. Those two had no idea which way he'd run after the botched robbery they had masterminded.

Slocum damned himself for throwing in with that pair. He hadn't known them but a few days, hitching up with them just outside Fort Davis. Their bragging hadn't impressed him, but the plan Barstow had for robbing the stagecoach looked to be a good one. Slocum had scouted it out himself and had seen that everything the other outlaw had said was right.

It should have been a cakewalk.

"There's no need for you to ride on, mister. Just put up your hands. We got you covered." The voice came from Slocum's left. Startled, he jerked around and saw a lawman on top of a huge boulder, six-shooter in his hand.

A dozen details blasted through Slocum's mind. The sheriff didn't have the backup—the posse was still behind them on the trail. The lawman was bluffing. It had to be that way. Slocum went for his Navy Colt and whipped it from the holster, thumb bringing back the hammer only halfway before letting it slip. The impact was enough to set off the round in the cylinder. Where the bullet went, Slocum didn't know or care. The unexpected resistance astonished the sheriff. He straightened in surprise, lost his footing, and then flailed wildly to keep from sliding down the side of the boulder.

Slocum didn't waste time watching his adversary. He kicked his mount into a gallop that lasted a hundred yards. When he felt the horse begin to tire rapidly, Slocum reined back. He heard gunshots and angry shouts behind him. The rest of the posse had caught up with the sheriff, who was warning them about the dangerous, crazy owlhoot they were chasing.

The sun was sinking in the west. Slocum knew the Rio Grande lay in that direction, but direct flight was cut off by a ridge of rock that seemed to rise straight out of the desert. He couldn't backtrack, not and expect to sneak past the sharp-eyed sheriff. Escaping the lawman a second time might be impossible now that he'd riled him by getting away like he had. No man appreciates being made to look like a fool.

Slocum had to keep riding away from the posse. Cutting toward the Rio Grande and the safety of Mexico would force him to scale the rocky crown rising to the west. To the east were more ridges of uneven hills blocking his path. Back north? Only a passel of guns waiting to ventilate him. Slocum pushed his horse as hard as he could straight south. Both tired rapidly, and Slocum fought to hold down rising panic.

He rode square into the mouth of a canyon. He had explored enough of the Big Bend to know that old rivers had cut some canyons and the wind and weather had carved others into boxes. He might get lucky again, for the third time in one day, and find this was an open-ended canyon. From the cries of glee behind him, he didn't think his luck was holding out. The posse was hooting and hollering because he was riding into a trap. A box canyon. And one, from the look of it, with enough big cottonwood trees to give them a good selection for a hanging.

Having no other choice, Slocum pushed ahead.

The sunlight quickly vanished behind the rise to the west, plunging much of the canyon into twilight. Slocum considered his chances of hiding, letting the posse rush past, then sneaking out. He rode to the side of the canyon with this in mind when he saw the sheriff and a dozen others rein back. The sheriff was a cagey bastard, and he wouldn't chance his victim evading him again. Half the posse formed a ragged line across the canyon's narrow mouth. To get away,

Slocum would have to slip past them.

All it would take was a single shot to bring the other lawmen running. From the way they chose their sentry points, they knew the lay of the land, and he didn't. Even darkness wasn't going to help him.

Posting the guards the way he did meant the sheriff knew this was a dead-end canyon, and he had Slocum boxed in.

"Come on out, mister. Surrender. You'll get a fair trial before we hang you!" The sheriff stood in his stirrups and cupped his hands to yell this dubious promise. If the dancing shadows hadn't made it a futile shot, Slocum would have knocked the man out of the saddle with a well-placed rifle slug.

To miss would be to reveal his location. Slocum hadn't been caught yet. As long as he kept moving, he might get away. He dismounted and led his tired horse deeper into the canyon, the east wall brushing his left arm. Keeping this close to the rock prevented attack from that direction, a small edge that was likely to turn against him when he reached the end of the canyon.

He walked quickly, hoping against hope that he wasn't trapped. When the canyon began curving around in the darkness, Slocum knew he was lost.

His gelding nickered and pulled at the reins in Slocum's hands. He gave the horse its head, wishing for a miracle. As far as the horse was concerned, a miracle had happened. It found a small pond cut in the rock from long years of water running off the canyon rim. Some small spring fed the pool from below. Slocum let the horse drink its fill. There wasn't any reason to keep it from the water and the sparse buffalo grass nearby. The clank of the posse told him he was going to have to find a spot and make his stand.

Slocum pulled his Winchester from its sheath, got a spare box of ammo from his saddlebags, and settled down on a rock, wondering how long it would be until the sheriff put a bullet through his head.

2

Slocum prepared to die.

He wasn't going to let any sheriff from some Podunk town that might not even have a name capture him. The few trees in the hot, dusty box canyon were sturdy enough for a hangman's noose to be tossed over a convenient limb. Slocum would rather die with a dozen slugs in his gut than go out kicking in the wind.

"You can't get away, mister. Come on and give up. We want to get on back to town before it gets much later."

Slocum paid scant attention to the sheriff's plea. It was nothing more than a crude ploy to provoke some response. They'd spot him easily enough when he started firing. The foot-long tongue of flame from the rifle's muzzle would be a beacon in the dusk. That made Slocum all the more determined to get a good first shot in. The more of the posse he killed or winged, the better it was for him.

Glancing over his shoulder, he saw his gelding had stopped drinking from the pool and had begun grazing on the grass. He hoped whoever took the horse didn't mistreat it. The animal had been a steady, reliable companion for him going on three months now.

He settled down and waited for the perfect target. Slocum saw dim, shadowy shapes flitting back and forth as the posse moved closer, not sure where he was and wary of a trap. Trying to figure the odds on getting out of the canyon gave Slocum a headache. It wasn't likely to happen by stealth, not with half the posse guarding the canyon's mouth.

"We got you now, mister. 'Less you want your hide filled with buckshot, toss down that six-shooter of yours." The sheriff moved fifty yards off, standing more boldly than the others. Slocum bit his lower lip, wondering what would happen to the posse if they lost their leader. A strong deputy might be able to take over. Confusion might scatter them, too.

He swung his rifle around, knowing the sheriff called out his threats and promises because he didn't have an inkling where Slocum was.

"You don't want to get left out here for the buzzards, now do you? Give up. I promise you a Christian burial back in town. We got a right fine cemetery in Fort Davis."

Slocum's finger pulled back gently on the trigger. It felt right. He recoiled when the rifle fired unexpectedly, the sure sign of a good squeeze. The sheriff let out a yelp and threw his hands into the air, thrashing about as if he'd stepped in an ant hill.

Slocum got off a second shot, but he knew this one missed by a country mile. The sheriff was already on his way to the ground, maybe not dead but certainly wounded. Slocum took some measure of pride in this. He had been one of the best snipers in the Confederate Army. Patience had always served him well, and now was no exception. He settled down to wait again, hoping that no one in the posse had seen the muzzle flash.

As he waited, thoughts of the past, of the war, of his dead brother and parents raced through his mind. Slocum wondered if this was what it meant to die. He had been in tough spots before but had never thought so much of them. His brother Robert had died during Pickett's Charge; the watch riding in his vest pocket was his only legacy.

And his parents. He hadn't seen them after the war. He had ridden with Quantrill's Raiders and had been ordered gut shot by Quantrill himself for complaining about the Lawrence, Kansas, raid. Bloody Bill Anderson had done the honors, laughing as he pulled the trigger. Slocum had been laid up, closer to death than life, when Anderson had been killed during the Centralia Massacre. Somehow, knowing the butcher was dead had given Slocum the strength to fight back.

He had gone home to Calhoun County, Georgia, to recover, only to find his parents had died months earlier. He had worked slowly, regaining his strength, settling into the life of a farmer, when a carpetbagger judge had taken a shine to Slocum's spread. No taxes had been paid during the war, so he'd have to confiscate the farm and sell the property to satisfy the government, the judge said. Slocum knew the man wanted to turn the land into a stud farm, thinking to raise purebred horses.

Slocum's troubles had begun that night when he rode away from his family's farm. Two new graves had been filled on the ridge, one holding a hired gun and the other the carpetbagger judge. No matter the reason or the justice of it, the law hated judge killers. This crime had dogged Slocum's trail ever since.

He wouldn't stand a chance if the sheriff lying out there, moaning to beat the band, ever riffled through a stack of wanted posters. Slocum let out a tiny chuckle. Even without the poster and the reward that seemed to grow with every new printing, that lawman wasn't likely to ever let Slocum out of this canyon alive. He had it in his head when he came after Slocum that he wasn't going home empty-handed.

Now he had been shot and his dignity, his authority, rested on bringing the criminal to swift justice.

Slocum squeezed off another round. This one flew straight and true. One of the posse seemed to melt like ice in the summer sun. His legs turned rubbery and he sank into himself like a deck of cards being shuffled. Slocum had seen that often enough. A clean kill. And with it, his luck ran out.

"There, there he is, Sheriff. Over to the left. He's got us in his sights! I seen him!"

Someone had spotted the muzzle flash. The echoes from the report still rattled back and forth through the canyon, confusing directions. But he had been located. Slocum cursed, but he knew it was inevitable. The canyon was broad—but it was also a dead end. They had him trapped and fighting out wasn't likely. He took the time to replace the three rounds in his Winchester's magazine.

"Circle, you mangy cayuses; cut him off so's he don't backtrack on us and get away," came the aggrieved sheriff's voice. Slocum almost laughed now. Gone was the placating tone, the false promises of quick justice and a decent burial. All the officer of the law wanted now was to show his men nobody could make a fool of him. No matter how this ended, Slocum had scored a minor victory.

Slocum retreated to his horse, thinking he might try galloping past the portion of the posse who had dismounted. How he would get past the guards at the canyon mouth was beyond him. They'd hear his horse's hooves, they'd hear the sheriff screeching that he was getting away. Slocum heaved a sigh. He might get them shooting at each other. That would be his only chance.

Just before he mounted, he saw an arc of fire in the twilight. The flaming arrow landed not ten feet from him. Then the sky lit with more flaming arrows. One followed another until Slocum saw the posse outlined by fires set in the tinder-dry brush.

He heaved another sigh. It wasn't enough that the sheriff was breathing down his neck. He had to run afoul of Lipan Apache, too. It hardly mattered how many ways he could die. He was going out with his Colt blazing.

He ducked as another arrow flew past his head. He wondered where the Indians were to get such an angle on him. The wild thought of throwing in with them passed as quickly as it came. The Lipan Apache were survivors. They had played their arch enemy the Comanche against the Spanish until the Comanche were dwindling in number, the Spanish were gone—and they were still riding the Texas plains. They'd never ally themselves with him.

Another arrow thudded into the ground just a few feet from Slocum. He hesitated. The arrows created confusion in the posse, and now it was his turn to wonder. Tied to the

shaft of this arrow was a white rag. At first he thought the
cloth had been dipped in coal oil and somehow the flames
had gone out. Then he looked more carefully and saw a
piece of paper poking out from under the white rag.

Slocum pulled the note free. A crude map had been
scratched on it. Slocum lined up the landmarks, then saw
a line of Xs marching through what might be a way out of
the box canyon.

Why the Lipan Apache would aid him against the law
wasn't something he was going to sit and ponder. Slocum
grabbed his horse's reins and tugged hard, getting the reluc-
tant gelding moving in the direction of what might be a
crack in the side of the box canyon.

It might also be a trap, though why the Indians would go
to such lengths to snare him wasn't obvious. The sheriff's
men still dodged the flaming arrows arcing down from
above. Slocum tried to trace their trajectory back to find
where the Indians were shooting from, but he couldn't.
There were too many possible spots along the ragged walls.
The Apaches might even be on the rim. A strong bowman
could send the storm of fire arrows a long way.

The horse saw the crevice before Slocum. He turned for
the narrow opening, then stopped, wondering again at his
fate. Why would the Lipan Apache save him?

The brief hesitation saved his life. The danger didn't lie
in the fissure, but behind. He heard a boot turn a stone.

Slocum swung around, his rifle leveling on a target. He
was blinded by the flash from a six-shooter; he fired in
reflex, though he didn't have a good target. He winced as
a streak burned past his left arm. The lawman getting the
drop on him had missed inflicting serious injury on him by
scant inches. And Slocum wasn't sure he had done anything
more than scare the deputy.

He considered what to do. Entering the crack in the
canyon wall was out of the question now. He'd be gunned
down, shot in the back, before he got ten yards. But how
many men did he face?

"I surrender!" he called, waiting to see what response
he got. "You hit me. I—I'm bleeding something fierce."

Slocum didn't cock his Winchester. The sound would have alerted the hidden lawman. He drew his Colt Navy and waited for movement, for sound, for anything that might give him a target.

"Come on out with your hands in the air where I can see 'em," came the quavering command. Slocum doubted the deputy was out of his teens. His voice cracked with strain.

"Can't," Slocum lied. "You hit me in the leg. Can't hardly move." He let his words trail off, as if he was losing too much blood to keep talking. "Here, here's my rifle." He croaked this out as he tossed his Winchester onto the sandy spit between him and the lawman.

Slocum didn't think the trick would work. And with an older, cagier, more experienced deputy it wouldn't have. But the youth poking his head out was hardly twenty. Slocum didn't want to kill him, but there didn't seem to be much choice. Given the chance, this boy would have laughed as Slocum swung with a rope around his neck.

"Here, over here," Slocum called. He was getting antsy. The flights of arrows had stopped—or if they continued, the arrows were no longer aflame. That meant the sheriff and the others in the posse would hazard a look around and finally be on his trail soon. He had to get away.

He glanced at the six-gun in his hand and knew he couldn't fire. It had nothing to do with the age of his opponent. Billy the Kid had been murdering men for most of his life by the time he was as old as the deputy. Slocum's caution came from not wanting to alert the sheriff to his getaway route.

Moving quickly, he ducked into deep shadow near the crevice. He waited for the deputy to blunder forward.

"Where'd you go? You ain't foolin' me, now are you?" the deputy demanded.

Slocum measured the distance between them, took a step forward and swung his Colt as hard as he could. The deputy sensed what was coming and let out a yelp that was cut off abruptly when the gun barrel smashed into the side of his head. The young man groaned and sank to his knees. He had a harder head than Slocum had anticipated. It took a second blow to put him out.

Panting from exertion, Slocum dragged the inert deputy back in the direction from which he'd come. It took only a few seconds to find his horse. The animal snorted and reared, fighting against its reins tied around a mesquite branch. Slocum dared the spines on the mesquite, yanked the reins free, and then heaved the deputy over the saddle so that he hung on either side. A quick swat to the horse's rump sent it racing into the night.

"There he goes!" Slocum shouted. "Get him. He's getting away!"

He saw orange blossoms grow in the darkness as others in the posse opened fire on the galloping horse. Slocum felt no satisfaction that the posse might be killing each other. All he wanted to do was get away. By the time the young deputy regained consciousness—if he survived—he would be far enough away that he might not be able to find where Slocum had ambushed him. Slocum hoped the deputy had never seen the crevice. Even if he had, he might not recognize it as a way out of the box canyon.

Slocum ran back to his gelding, retrieved his fallen Winchester, then began pulling his skittish horse toward the fissure. The horse balked and tried to rear. Slocum forced himself to stay calm in spite of the growing sense of urgency to get away. The sheriff wasn't going to be decoyed for long by the unfortunate deputy and his racing horse. When he figured out what Slocum had done and backtracked, he'd find the crevice and be madder than a rained-on rooster.

"Whoa, easy, old boy," he said, hanging on tight to the reins. The walls of the fissure rubbed both of Slocum's shoulders. He didn't cotton much to close places, but he could endure it if it meant getting away from the law. But the horse wasn't inclined to go along easily. Slocum finally gentled the horse enough to get it walking. When it reared again, he knew what he had to do.

A horse will run back into a burning building. As far as Slocum was concerned, that's what the gelding wanted to do by backing out of the chasm and returning to the box canyon. He whipped off his bandanna and tied it over the horse's eyes. The animal spooked a mite, then settled down as Slocum talked softly to it.

The going wasn't easy through the tight space, but it wasn't anywhere near as difficult as it had been with the balky horse behind him.

For what seemed an eternity, Slocum walked through the darkness, aware of only a narrow strip of stars high above him in the sky. The sheer rock walls cut off his view of most of the sky. Now and then a cloud drifted directly overhead and plunged the fissure into complete darkness. Slocum felt as if he had been trapped inside some black box, no light reaching his eyes. If it hadn't been for the law so hot behind him, he'd have considered just standing and waiting for first light before continuing.

He kept walking, not wanting to spend more time in the crack through the rocks than he had to. After another twenty minutes, his shoulders no longer touched the walls. Another five, and the fissure was wide enough to allow him to walk beside his horse. Slocum chanced removing the blindfold. The horse reared and then settled down, more comfortable now that there was some space to move about.

Slocum moved faster now, more comfortable with the broadening crevice. He took a deep breath of fresh air when he reached the edge of the crevice and paused. Something was wrong. He figured out what it was about the same time he heard the metallic click of a cartridge being chambered into a rifle.

Somebody's campfire had died down. They had burned mesquite and the distinctive odor lingered in the crisp, clean desert air. Slocum had recognized it too late.

In a half-circle around him stood four men with their rifles leveled and ready to fire. He had left one trap and walked smack dab into another.

3

"Shoot 'im, Adam!" cried one man, his hand shaking on the rifle he held. "Cut the bastard down where he stands!"

Slocum's mind raced. He couldn't get back into the narrow fissure fast enough. Even if he tried, his horse was likely to be a target. Without the gelding, he wouldn't make it a day in the hot West Texas desert. He couldn't run. And he didn't see how he could fight men with rifles already trained on him.

"Wait!" Slocum tried to distract them before they filled him full of holes. He cursed his bad luck running from one posse and landing smack dab in the middle of another.

"Yeah, wait a second before you go to shooting," came a slow drawl, from deep shadow, that Slocum almost recognized. "We don't want to go shooting a man who is going to help us, now do we, gents?" From the shadows emerged the fourth man. He grinned broadly but didn't shift his aim away from Slocum's gut.

"It's been a spell, Jenks," Slocum said. He didn't relax, but now he knew he wasn't likely to be gunned down. He had ridden with Adam Jenks a year or two back. He had never thought much about the outlaw, other than that it was safe enough turning his back on him. That said more for the man's character than anything else Slocum could think of.

"Slocum here is our answer to a big dilemma," Jenks said,

17

moving forward. "That is, unless this here cat's changed his spots since we rode together."

"You rode with this owlhoot?" The man who wanted to cut Slocum down looked puzzled. It didn't take Slocum but an instant to realize who the brains was in this outfit, and it wasn't the man asking the question. At this, Slocum almost laughed. He'd never thought of Adam Jenks as a deep thinker. He certainly wasn't overly ambitious or good at planning. That meant whatever the outlaw was up to wouldn't amount to a hill of beans. Jenks had always been a penny ante kind of player.

And that suited Slocum just fine. Jenks wasn't likely to have the law breathing down his neck.

"That I did, that I did. Slocum and me was the best of buddies, weren't we, John?" Jenks threw his arm around Slocum's shoulder as if they had been through hell together. Slocum couldn't remember one decent robbery they'd accomplished, nor could he spin a tall tale about daring breakouts or skin-of-the-teeth getaways. He doubted if the entire take from all their robberies when they'd ridden in the Gus Goslin gang amounted to five hundred dollars. Split five ways over a period of six months, that made for a piss-poor living. He could have done better punching cows.

"We had our moments," Slocum said cautiously. He glanced over his shoulder in the direction of the crevice. "We'd better be moving on. We can reminisce about old times later."

"You got the law after you, now do you, John?" Jenks smiled even more broadly, making Slocum look around to see if any of the men with Jenks had badges pinned on their shirts. None did. And the mention of a posse after him made the other three noticeably uneasy. Jenks hadn't changed his profession, as many second-rate highwaymen did. In many towns, being sheriff wasn't much different from holding up the afternoon stagecoach, and was a damned sight less risky.

"There's a bit of misunderstanding about yesterday afternoon and what happened to the stage," Slocum said, not wanting to fully explain. Slocum had no idea why the sheriff was so tenacious. Whatever the reason, he wanted it to remain a complete mystery to him—and from as far away as possible.

"Do tell. Well, gents, let's get our camp moved down the road a ways. John here's going to tell us all about it. Truly he is." Again Jenks hugged Slocum close as if they were long lost brothers. Such familiarity made Slocum wary. He didn't remember Adam Jenks as a particularly friendly cuss. He wasn't the back-shooting type, but he had never gone out of his way to be friendly, either.

The others lowered their rifles and hastily packed their meager belongings. Jenks kicked the campfire apart and sheathed his rifle in its saddle scabbard. Slocum waited silently, wondering if he ought to just slip into the night. He could be a mile off before Jenks even noticed. And from all he remembered, the man wasn't much of a tracker. Fact was, the man wasn't good at much of anything.

"We do need you, John. We finally got the big one in our grasp." Jenks held up a grimy paw and squeezed, as if crushing the life from a small animal. "We can do it ourselves, but with you—well, it's a done deal."

"Never saw a robbery that was a done deal," Slocum said. "There's always risk."

"That's because you rode with losers like Goslin before now. What did that gent know of finding good banks to rob or stagecoaches to hold up? Pennies, all we ever got with him was pennies. We wasted our time, John, we truly did."

"But not this time?" Slocum saw that the others had mounted and looked to Jenks for direction. That was both good and bad in a gang. Having a leader control his men was essential, but these three didn't seem to be able to wipe their noses without getting Jenks's approval.

No matter how good a plan, something always went wrong during a robbery. Slocum liked to have men who could think on their feet, who'd do what had to be done without being told. That spelled the difference between enjoying the fruits of a robbery and swinging from a gallows in the dawn's weak light.

They rode slowly through the darkness, the bright stars above giving off enough light to see by. The Milky Way stretched in a diamond-studded arch that made Slocum want to follow it—away from the likes of Adam Jenks and his feckless gang.

"Hear me out before you decide that it's all bullshit," Jenks said earnestly. "How far do you reckon we ought to go to be safe from the law?"

Slocum wasn't sure there was enough distance, even in Texas. The desert turned cold at night, but it was a hot wind blowing at the back of his neck. That lawman hadn't given up.

"I reckon he has delusions of being a Ranger. You'd think I killed his dog instead of just sticking up a stage."

"Get much from it?" asked Jenks, eager to hear how Slocum had made out.

Slocum bit his lower lip. Barstow and Dunphy had crossed him. He was sure of that. But why? How? The miserable few dollars they'd gotten from the strongbox couldn't possibly make up for having Slocum track them down to the ends of the earth to get his revenge. The money was important; getting even with those two sidewinders was even more essential to Slocum's peace of mind.

"Nothing," he said. "The two with me got away with the money."

Adam Jenks laughed and Slocum wanted to throttle him for it. "That's rich, John, truly it is. You stick up a stage-coach, and they get the money and you get the law on your trail. Well, the boys and me got a sweet deal in the works. Nothing can go wrong, if you throw in with us on it."

"Why do you need me if this is such a clean robbery?"

"Intelligence," Jenks said.

For a moment Slocum misunderstood.

"You know, John, like the cavalry does. Intelligence. Information. Scouting. We need somebody to get us the news we need to pull off the robbery as slick as a whis-tle."

"Why can't you get it for yourselves?" Slocum listened

with half an ear. Whatever Jenks had going, Slocum wasn't
interested.

"Well, they know us a mite too well over in Van Eyck."

Slocum tried to remember the names of the towns in
the area. Van Eyck didn't sound familiar. Fort Davis and
Alpine were about the only places he'd recognize. Maybe
Marfa or Van Horne, but they were farther north, up toward
El Paso.

"What's so all-fired important about Van Eyck?" he
asked, as much to keep Jenks talking as to find out what
the planned robbery was.

"You sure it's all right to tell him everything, Adam?"
asked a man riding on the outlaw's other side. "Me and Ed
and Pecos don't know him and—"

"Johnny, my boy, Slocum's a square-shooter. Me and
him rode with the Gus Goslin bunch. I told you about those
days."

"Well, sure, yeah, but—"

"We need him in Van Eyck so's we know when to swoop
in and take the payroll. You go on up ahead with the others
and let me and Slocum hash this out."

The man obeyed sullenly. This was as close to thinking
as he was likely to come.

"You got to work with what you can find, John. Truly
now, don't you find that to be so?" Jenks looked at him, but
Slocum stared straight ahead, thoughts of revenge dancing
in his head. Barstow and Dunphy hadn't gotten much from
the robbery, but it would all be his. They had no call to
double-cross him. The notion that they'd do such a thing
rankled more as he rode.

"You want in on this, John? It's better than any stagecoach robbery. Truly it is."

"What? Oh, I don't know, Jenks. I'm thinking it's time
for me to head east. Maybe to Fort Worth, or even New
Orleans. Been a spell since I was there. There's always
money flowing through any port city along the Mississippi.
And the gambling's good."

"You need money, John. You do, for such a fine city.
What good is it wandering the French Quarter without two

nickels to rub together? They didn't leave you anything, and if I remember you a'right, you're not the kind who forgets."

"What's your point?" Slocum saw a branch in the road ahead. If he took the northern fork, he'd head up toward Fort Davis. That might be dangerous since he didn't know where the sheriff on his trail hailed from. Riding into the very town the sheriff called home might be a big mistake. But the south fork didn't look to go far enough in that direction. Maybe it edged on toward San Antonio.

That was a safer direction, Slocum decided. He said nothing to Jenks and turned his gelding's head onto the southern road. Jenks and the others trotted with him. Slocum cursed his bad luck. He'd hoped they would go in the other direction.

"It's a big one, John, truly the biggest payroll I ever heard about."

"How big?" Slocum asked, more interested. "And who's it for?"

"The railroad workers, down south of Van Eyck. There's a railhead going in somewhere nearby, but nobody knows exactly where. Until then, Van Eyck's bank holds the monthly payroll. More'n two hundred Irishmen working on laying down steel, John. Two hundred! That's a heap of money residing in the bank, and it's all just waiting for us to withdraw." Jenks laughed and added, "At gunpoint."

"Any payroll like that would be guarded, and even if Van Eyck is some jerkwater town—"

"The railroad's bypassing them. That's the rich part, John. I don't reckon the local law'd be too upset losing the railroad's money. They wanted the company to come smack through the center of town. As it stands, being bypassed means Van Eyck will be a ghost town."

"So the people in Van Eyck don't much care if the railroad loses its payroll," Slocum said, exasperated. "That doesn't mean the railroad bosses will roll over and play dead."

"Don't expect them to. We can be long gone by the time word reaches them. John, there's one whale of a lot of money in that tin can of a bank, and it's just begging for us to come take it!"

It was never this easy, and Slocum knew it, but the lure of a railroad payroll nudged his greed enough to keep him quiet. Jenks would try selling him on the robbery, and he might find out the outlaw wasn't blowing smoke this time. Even the stupidest of men can luck out and stumble over a perfect robbery.

"I've got other business," Slocum said.

"The two what double-crossed you? They'll keep, John. Think how much nicer it'd be huntin' them down with a wad of greenbacks in your pocket big enough to choke a cow. That's the kind of money we're talking about here."

"How much?"

Adam Jenks swallowed hard. "Can't be sure. That's one thing we need to know. You'd have to nose around in Van Eyck and get a sense of it, just to let us know if the risk is worth it."

Slocum saw nothing wrong with this. In fact, such good sense on Jenks's part surprised him. If the payoff wasn't big enough, why bother taking the risk?

"Why me? You got three men with you. They can belly up to a bar and get drunk and listen as well as I can."

"Well, John, it's like this. We had a little run-in with the fine folks in Van Eyck."

"How little?"

"Enough so's they'd make us uncomfortable returning. That's why we need somebody they don't know, somebody who can figure out everything we'll need."

Slocum heard what the outlaw was saying. They wanted someone to do the scouting, to find out how much firepower might be arrayed against them in the bank and out, and to plan the robbery itself. Jenks had stumbled across the payroll and wanted someone else to do the hard work.

"If I say the money's not worth it, you'll just walk away?" Slocum asked.

"Reckon so, but the payroll is going to be huge. Two hundred men. An entire month. Hell, John, even if they pay those dumb Micks a dollar a day, that's well nigh two thousand dollars. And the foremen and others get more."

"Two thousand split five ways," Slocum mused. That would get him quite a way down the road—or keep him going for months, long enough to find Barstow and Dunphy. That appealed to him more than the lure of his cut of four hundred dollars.

"There's more likely to be in the bank, too. There's supply money. I heard rumors it's going to come in at the same time."

"What supply money? You mean for goods from the general store, things like that?"

"Yes!" Adam Jenks almost fell from the saddle as he turned and waved his arms excitedly. "There's no telling how much that'll be. Most railroads ship in their goods on the track they've already laid. Not this one. They want to keep the local folks happy so they're buying from each town as they go, especially the ones they're passing by."

"Just to keep the people happy about living in a new ghost town?" Slocum said. That hardly sounded like any railroad company he knew, but maybe some big magnate took it into his head to do things right for a change. It would certainly keep the peace better than just pulling the rug out from under a town and letting everyone fall.

"Maybe more than two thousand," Slocum said, "and all I have to do is tell you the money's actually in the bank?" This seemed too easy to be true. There had to be more to it. Jenks didn't disappoint him.

"That and give us an idea how many guns we'd be facing, maybe decide on the best time, things like that. We'd need to know everything what goes on inside the bank. I tell you truly, John, this is one sweet robbery. It's going to make us all rich!"

Whatever Adam Jenks's other failings were, being a good liar wasn't one of them. Slocum didn't reckon the outlaw could ever muster this much enthusiasm for something he didn't believe was sound. He might be dead wrong, he might have his information turned all inside out, he might not know a hawk from a handsaw, but Slocum didn't think so. Not this time. It was damned hard to ignore a railroad going past a town, and workers did demand payment now and again.

The only fly in the ointment Slocum could see might be how the money was protected. The local sheriff might not care if the railroad was robbed blind, but someone on the railroad did—and most West Texas banks looked more like fortresses than clapboard buildings. The banker might not cotton to having everything removed forcibly from his vault since there'd be more taken than just railroad money.

But that meant there would be even more riding high in John Slocum's shirt pocket.

"Well, John, what about it? Are you game?"

"I'll sleep on it," Slocum said, but thoughts of being rich warmed him against the cold desert night. And with that money came freedom to find Barstow and Dunphy. Nobody double-crossed him and got away with it. Nobody.

4

"You know what to do, John. This is going to be good. Truly, it is. Me and the boys will be waiting for you to tell us when to come take out all that money!" Adam Jenks's enthusiasm was wearing on Slocum. For two days they had drifted slowly toward Van Eyck, following a course designed to let Slocum know if the sheriff was still hot on his trail. Going through the crevice at the rear of the box canyon had lost the sheriff, but the Apaches?

That bothered him almost as much as the sheriff. Slocum hadn't seen so much as a feather showing the Lipan were near. The shower of flaming arrows had come from somewhere, but Slocum didn't know where. A single war party might have camped on the canyon rim and taken it into their heads that the sheriff and his posse were there to return them to a reservation. Or maybe they just wanted some sport and had shot the fire arrows at the white men. But Slocum didn't find any trace of them, something that worried him more than it should.

The aimless wandering had also failed to give him any clue to where Barstow and Dunphy had gone. It was as if the earth had opened up and swallowed them whole. If it had happened that way, it'd save Slocum the trouble of digging graves for the pair.

"Van Eyck's just over the rise, John. Go on in and nose around, tell us what you—" Jenks shut up when he saw the coldness in Slocum's green eyes. This wasn't a man to gush to about a robbery.

"You've told me where you'll be camped," Slocum said. "Shouldn't take more than a day to find out when the payroll's due and how many guards the bank will have on it."

"Good luck, John. See you then, right, gents?" Jenks spoke louder now for the benefit of his three followers. Johnny, Pecos, and Ed had drifted more like ghosts than men, never doing or saying anything unless they were told, making Slocum think they were as useless as a four card flush.

Slocum nodded brusquely and turned his gelding's head toward the road leading into Van Eyck. He didn't know what to expect from the small Texas town, but it had to be more peace and quiet than he'd gotten riding with Adam Jenks. The man had turned into a magpie, chattering endlessly about how rich they'd all be.

If Slocum thought he'd find quiet in a sleepy town, he quickly discovered how wrong he was. Banners strung across the dusty street flapped in the hot wind, and men stood on boxes at opposite sides of the street, yelling at one another. Slocum reined back and tried to figure out what was happening. There seemed more heat than light in the discussion, if the pissing match could be called that. He rode past, working his way through the crowd that had gathered in front of each man and hoped that one wouldn't start shooting at the other. It seemed like that kind of gathering.

He dismounted in front of a saloon and looked around, trying to find where the law had staked out spots to observe. This many people would bring out the sheriff and a half dozen deputies, just to watch the ruckus if not for real work. Slocum frowned when he didn't see any badges, either in the crowd or along the boardwalks lining the wide dirt street going smack dab through the center of Van Eyck.

His gaze slowed and fixed on the town's bank halfway down the street. It stood by itself, no buildings on either side. And he didn't like what he saw. First impressions might be wrong, but this time Slocum didn't think so. The town was the usual West Texas mixture of adobe and rickety clapboard, with an occasional two-story frame building to show that some rich citizen had rustled up enough lumber to rise above the common herd below.

The bank stood impressively with its brick exterior and sturdy wood pillars. The windows were covered with bars thicker than those in the Detroit Federal Penitentiary. And the two men pacing back and forth on the boardwalk carried sawed-off shotguns, enough firepower to cut a crowd in half. Slocum didn't have to venture though the heavy portals to know they carried massive locks, or that security inside the Bank of Van Eyck was equally impressive.

An army would have trouble busting in. Getting money out of the vault was going to take even more effort. A cannon or a Gatling gun might breach the front doors. Dynamite for the still unseen vault—would it take as much as a case? More? Slocum shuddered as he thought how hard this robbery was going to be. Adam Jenks hadn't done any scouting, letting himself be blinded by the vague promise of a tremendous railroad payroll.

"Know how you feel," a man sitting in front of the saloon said, staring hard at Slocum.

"How's that?" Slocum asked. He hadn't wanted his attention on the bank to be so obvious, and the man doing the talking didn't have the look of a rival for the contents of the vault. The grizzled old galoot had rocked back, bracing the edge of his chair against the saloon wall. He scratched his stubbled chin and then shook his head.

"Reckoned you were thinkin' what a poor town this must be, the folks all arguin' over the sheriff like they are."

Slocum's attention turned away from the bank and back to the two crowds. The speakers had whipped both sides into a frenzy of cheering and jeering. He still couldn't make head nor tail out of the reason for such behavior, especially in the increasingly hot sun. The wind was fierce enough to sear the hair off a bull's hide, but the sun baked everything under it, including people's brains.

"What's the sheriff done to get them so riled?" Slocum asked, wondering if this might be a way into the bank. A town without a sheriff wasn't helpless any more than a docile dog with a mouthful of teeth was harmless, but the discord might give him a small edge.

The old man laughed. "He done the worst he could. He upped and quit!"

"Van Eyck doesn't have a sheriff?" Slocum looked back toward the bank. A third guard had joined the two on patrol in front of the bank. He looked up and saw a fourth man on the roof with a rifle. The way he carried it made Slocum think he knew how to use it. The bank looked more and more like a fortress. When two women were stopped at the door and their purses searched, Slocum knew getting in and out would take more than the three men Jenks had riding with him.

"If'n you're worryin' about the bank, there's no call for that," the man said, rocking forward and putting all four legs onto the walk. The chair tottered slightly, one chair leg shorter than the others. "Banker Mulholland is a fraidy-cat, he is. Ever since he heard tell of that railroad going past the town, he's done God knows what to get them to change their minds."

"What railroad?" Slocum asked, probing for more information.

"Won't see so much as a steel spike in Van Eyck," the man said. He coughed and wiped his lips, looking expectantly at Slocum. The hint was dropped and Slocum picked up on it.

"What say we go inside out of the wind and have a drink? First one's on me."

"Best offer I ever heard," the old man said, preceding Slocum into the saloon. To Slocum's surprise the man didn't belly up to the bar but went around it, fished under the backbar until he found a bottle filled with smoky amber liquid. He took down two shot glasses and sloshed some of the whiskey into them, his eye gleaming at the sight of such fine bourbon.

"You the barkeep?" Slocum asked as he lifted the glass. The aroma from the liquor told him this wasn't trade whiskey mixed with gunpowder and rusty nails to give it body. It might actually be the Kentucky bourbon it promised on the faded label.

"Barkeep, piano player, bouncer now that the sheriff's left town, sometimes I even think I'm the owner." He tossed back the whiskey and rolled it around his mouth with obvious gusto, then let it slide down his gullet, a smile of contentment on his face. "I save this for special occasions."

"Me buying you a drink is special? You must have a town full of skinflints," said Slocum, amused. He let the fine bourbon slide past his own tongue and puddle warmly in his belly. It had been a month of Sundays since he'd tasted this whiskey's equal.

"I got a feeling you're what this town needs. Don't go asking why I think that. I got the second sight. Always have."

Slocum laughed at this. He was precisely what Van Eyck *didn't* need now that their sheriff had taken a powder.

"Yes, sir, you got the look of a man wanting to find a place to call home. A spot to hang his hat. And from the worn handle on that Colt, you're mighty handy with a six-shooter."

"Might be bringing trouble to town," Slocum said.

"My second sight doesn't go wrong, no, sir, it don't," the saloon owner said. "You're gonna put an end to the lawlessness in Van Eyck."

"Now why would I go and do a damnfool thing like that?" Slocum asked. "I have no interest in getting shot up." Even as the words left his mouth, gunfire came from the street. The two crowds had turned ugly and antagonistic toward each other. Angry shouts sounded, followed by more gunshots.

"They been at it ever since Sheriff Dawkins moved on," the barkeep said. "One side blames the other for not givin' him enough money. The other blames the first bunch for givin' him too much. Seems he might have upped and made off with the civic improvement money."

"Civic improvement money?"

"The town listened to Banker Mulholland about gettin' the railroad through here. They raised well nigh a thousand dollars to influence the railroad to come to town."

"You mean they raised bribe money."

"Ain't a one in town what'd call it that, 'cept the few honest ones. Anyway, seems the money is gone and so is the sheriff. Can't say one is related to the other, but a suspicious man might say that."

"Have they tried tracking Dawkins?"

This amused the old man immensely. He laughed so hard tears came to his eyes. He wiped them away with a dirty bar rag, then poured Slocum and himself another drink.

"This one's on me," he said, still chuckling. "Best laugh I've had in a spell. Dawkins went over to the railroad and bought a goldanged ticket on their road. He might be in Saint Looie by now."

"What'd the banker think of having his money stolen?"

"Mulholland don't much care. He's got the railroad money coming and going through his bank. He makes a durn sight more off that than any paltry sum of money raised by the town. Don't figure he was too happy since it made him look a bit stupid, but he's getting rich, so what's he care?"

"You don't care much for Mulholland, do you?"

"Don't care much for any human being. Had a dog once I really liked, but that was years ago. He upped and died on me, the mangy wretch. Never did forgive him."

More gunfire outside made Slocum turn and stare through the saloon's double doors. The crowds were throwing rocks at each other. He didn't see who was doing the shooting, but nobody seemed much afraid of being cut down.

"How long's this been going on?"

"The name-calling and shooting? Too long," the barkeep said. "That's why we need somebody in this town who can grab 'em by the scruffs of their dirty necks and shake 'em like a terrier with a rat."

"Not interested," Slocum said, amused at the notion of anyone thinking he was cut out to be a sheriff. He had spent more time in jails than many lawmen, but it had always been on the wrong side of the bars. And he'd never stayed a second longer than he had to, breaking out at the first chance.

"You are thinkin' of stayin' a spell, though. I see it in your eyes."

"Guilty on that count," Slocum said. "I thought to put some of my money in the bank, but the way the guards search everybody—" He let the sentence trail off.

"Mulholland don't do that all the time. He's getting nervous over a big payroll coming in sometime soon. Mostly, he's only got one or two guards posted there, what with the sheriff gone and all." The barkeep shook his grizzled head. "He's not going to lose any money from his bank, no sir."

"Much obliged," Slocum said, indicating the drink. He dropped a silver cartwheel on the bar for the first drinks. Like any barkeep, the man's hand moved faster than thought, making the money vanish.

"If you're going to stay, let me give you a word of advice. Don't go takin' sides. Dawkins was a fool, but he was a good enough man to be Van Eyck's sheriff. Arguing over him and the lost money only wastes time and annoys the hell out of folks who don't agree with you."

Slocum tipped his hat, smiled, and left the saloon. He sidled along the front of the saloon, crossed the street, and avoided the brawl growing in the middle of the street. Losing money wasn't something anybody took in stride, no matter how much you had, but Slocum couldn't figure why the town was making such a big deal out of the sheriff stealing their "civic development" money.

The reasons for their distemper had to run deeper. Maybe they knew Van Eyck was doomed now that the railroad had passed them by. Maybe there just wasn't much else to do in the town.

Slocum walked slowly down the street, studying the buildings, trying to get an idea how to attack the bank.

The closest structure to the bank was Mrs. Parman's Boardinghouse, rooms by the week or month, or so said the simple sign in the front yard. A smaller sign underneath said NO VACANCIES. Slocum mentally positioned a sniper on the boardinghouse's upper floor or on its roof to take out guards at the bank. It wouldn't be a hard shot, but what happened then? Jenks and his gang still had to get inside the brick fortress.

The other side of the bank didn't offer any more inspiration for breaching the walls and emptying the vault. A dry goods store and a veterinary office weren't good for staging an assault. Too many people came and went and word would get over to the army guarding the bank. He'd have to look around back, but he doubted it held any more promise for easy entry than any other spot he could see.

Slocum hesitated on the walk outside the bank. The two shotgun-toting guards positioned themselves on either side, the muzzles of their deadly weapons swinging in his direction. They ignored the ruckus in the street in favor of keeping a close watch on him.

"How do I open an account?" he asked.

"You got to leave your six-gun with us if you go inside. Them's the rules."

Slocum handed over his ebony-handled Navy Colt, feeling naked. He went inside and looked around quickly before anyone could accost him. It was as he feared. The exterior of the bank was well guarded. Inside was even worse. He saw small loopholes cut in the walls on either side of the tellers' cages. The glint of steel plate came through the small cuts, showing armor behind the wood facade. Two men with rifles could hold off a frontal attack forever behind those barricades.

And getting back to the vault presented problems of its own. The heavy door of the Chubb safe would take more than a couple sticks of dynamite to blow. An entire case might not be too much, even if Slocum thought the job could be done with less. Holes would have to be drilled to direct the force of the explosion against the vault door's hinges. It wasn't hard to do, but it would take time.

"Help you, sir?" asked a teller. The man squinted at him from under a green visor.

Slocum started an account in the bank with a ten-dollar greenback he had folded in his shirt pocket. It was a sizable portion of the money he had, but he decided it was worth handing over to the bank's safekeeping just to see what he was up against. By having the account established, getting in to look the place over later—nearer the time the payroll was to be delivered—would be easier.

"I do declare," came an elderly woman's voice from the door. "You'd think I was a criminal."

"Just following the rules, ma'am," one of the shotgun guards outside said. They searched her purse before letting her in. She went to the other teller's cage and took out five dollars from her account. Slocum was slower to finish, needing to fill out too much paperwork for his liking. The woman put her money into a small cloth drawstring purse and left.

"There you are," the teller said, finishing. He shoved a small book toward Slocum. "Regular deposits mean regular income. We pay two percent on deposits." When Slocum just looked at him, the teller explained, "At the end of the year, every dollar you have with us, we give you two cents more. You leave that ten dollars in and next year we'll give you twenty cents for doing nothing."

"Thanks," Slocum said, shoving the small book into his shirt pocket. He stopped at the door to retrieve his pistol. Just reaching the street let him breathe a little easier. The thought that armed guards lurked behind those steel plates made him jumpy.

The woman who had left a few seconds before him was crossing the street, heading toward the dry goods store. Slocum watched as two men came swinging out of the barbershop, joking and shoving each other. They stopped when they saw the woman. One said something, and they both laughed. Then they made a beeline for her.

Slocum hesitated to act. This wasn't his concern. The entire town ought to have a sheriff to keep the peace. But

Sheriff Dawkins had robbed them blind and was maybe a thousand miles away.

"Whatcha got in there, little lady?" asked one ruffian. He grabbed for the woman's purse. She pulled it in close to her body and tried to turn away. The other man seized her by the shoulders and spun her around so hard she fell to her knees in the dirt.

It wasn't Slocum's fight. But he acted. Quick, long strides brought him to the woman's side as she fought to keep the two men from taking her purse.

"You'd look mighty foolish carrying around a woman's purse," Slocum said in a level voice.

"Who the hell asked you?" blazed one man. He stepped back, his hand slipping toward his holstered six-shooter.

He froze when he saw the tombstones reflected in Slocum's cold green eyes.

"Get on out of town, why don't you? Or you can stay. I hear they still got room in their potter's field," Slocum said.

The second man started for the six-gun thrust into his waistband. Slocum didn't even bother drawing. He swung, balanced on the balls of his feet. He felt the man's belly giving way around his rock-hard fist. Air gushed from the petty thief's lungs, and he folded like a bad poker hand. Slocum spun, his hand flashing for his Colt. He had it out, aimed and cocked, before the other man cleared leather.

"Leave town on your feet—or feet first. It doesn't matter to me which way you go," Slocum said.

"Didn't mean nothing by it, mister. Honest!" The man helped up his still gasping partner and they backed away. When they were a safe distance off, Slocum let the hammer down gently and returned his six-shooter to its cross-draw holster. Only then did he see quite a crowd had gathered.

"You all right, ma'am?" he asked, helping the woman to her feet.

"Yes, thank you. I—"

"Mrs. Parman, are you all right? They didn't hurt you, did they? I came when I saw them from your parlor. The ruffians!"

He hadn't known he was rescuing the proprietress of the small boardinghouse he had passed just before going into Mulholland's bank. And he hadn't known women were as pretty as the young woman who rushed to Mrs. Parman's aid. The smile the blond gave him was brighter than the West Texas sun and turned him hotter inside than the fine whiskey the barkeep had poured.

When she reached out and touched his arm lightly, it seemed as if everyone else in Van Eyck had vanished and the two of them were alone in the world. Then the spell was broken, the blond helped Mrs. Parman to her feet, and they started back toward the boardinghouse. But she turned and gave Slocum a parting smile filled with thanks and promise.

5

Slocum watched the vision of blond loveliness drift away, carried off on the tide of the crowd closing in around him. He tried to follow, to say something more, but the crowd wouldn't let him.

"That's about the bravest thing I ever saw. Those two owlhoots were cold-blooded killers. They probably done kilt old man Burnside out on the Rolling J Ranch, though nobody ever proved it," someone in the crowd said.

"It's nothing," Slocum said, trying to push his way through them. He failed. They kept crowding him.

"Anybody could have done it," he said.

They crowded closer, reaching out to touch him like Sioux warriors counting coup.

"You are a true hero, mister," a woman said. "You deserve a reward or something."

"Who was that?" Slocum asked, standing on tiptoe and trying to see where the blond had gone. The crowd kept him pinned. He thought about taking his pistol out and firing it into the air to see if he could scatter them.

"Her? Why that's old lady Parman. She owns the only decent boardinghouse in town."

"The blond?" Slocum was astounded.

"Her? No, no, the woman you saved from being robbed. That other's the Widow Clairmont."

"A widow, is she?" Slocum asked. Van Eyck was looking

better to him by the moment, and he couldn't forget the hot gaze laden with promise the blond had given him as she helped the owner of the boardinghouse back home. If the bank proved a bust, there might be other rewards to be had by staying in the small town, at least for a spell.

"She's a nice woman," someone else said. To Slocum all the faces in the crowd blurred into one. He wasn't used to being surrounded by so many people, and he was beginning to feel cornered. He pushed back and they gave him some breathing space.

"You lookin' for a job, mister?" came a voice Slocum remembered. "Why not stay in Van Eyck and be sheriff?"

Slocum turned and saw the grizzled owner of the saloon. The old galoot smiled a ragged grin in his direction, as if saying, "I told you so."

"Don't go shootin' off your danged mouth like that, Fenneman," snapped a man at the rear of the crowd. "We got to have an election to get our new sheriff. We don't just give it out like it was candy to a young'n. We got to do things right."

"Do things right?" Fenneman mocked. "The only way you'd consider right is if you got to be sheriff, March."

"I got a right. Anybody in Van Eyck's got a right to run for sheriff—but not this fellow. He just breezed into town. What's anybody know about him? Maybe this was staged. He might have hired them to turn tail and run like whipped dogs. It's downright convenient, don't you think?" March pushed his way through the crowd, giving Slocum a look at the man who wanted to be the new sheriff.

Slocum wasn't impressed. March looked as if he spent more time at the dinner table than he did doing anything else. He had a gut that hung over his belt by quite a few inches, but cinched tight around his middle was a hand-tooled Mexican gun belt. Slocum moved to get a closer look at the side arm in it. He decided March was all bluster and blow. Spots of rust were clearly visible in the hot sun. For metal to rust in West Texas took more than a tad of neglect.

"Nothing says a sheriff's got to be a voting citizen of the

town," Fenneman went on, seeing the crowd was shifting in his direction. Slocum wondered if the people of Van Eyck did anything but harangue each other all day long. He hadn't seen much that was productive being done since he rode in. Except the bank.

Thought and great effort had gone into making it impregnable.

"What's your name, son?" asked Fenneman. It took Slocum a second to realize the saloon owner was talking to him. He mumbled his name, wondering if he'd made a bad mistake. The wanted posters always seemed to show up at the wrong time. Judge-killing wasn't considered a sport in too many towns that called themselves civilized.

"Mr. Slocum here is a fine, upstanding example of the kind of folks what settled Van Eyck. He held back the lawless tide washing over us when he defended Mrs. Parman." This got a rise from the crowd. Everyone knew the owner of the boardinghouse and apparently liked her.

The one Slocum wanted to get to know better was the Widow Clairmont.

"He stood up when others among us"—Fenneman glared at March—"stood by and watched those goldanged thieves beset her! Who deserves to be sheriff?" The roar that went up from the crowd scared Slocum. He thought they were going to hoist him to their shoulders, bounce him around, and then pin a star on his shirt.

"The election!" wailed March. "There's got to be an election. You said so yourself, Fenneman."

"There'll be a fair election, March, but you won't be running unopposed. Slocum'll run against you."

Slocum tried to protest, but no one paid him any mind.

"He ain't paid the registration fees," growled March. "He can't get his name on the ballot without ponying up the fees."

Slocum thought this sounded more like a county fair than an election, but Fenneman wasn't going to be thwarted easily. He held up his hands and said in a voice pitched just low enough to force everyone to concentrate to hear him, "I'll foot the bill for Mr. Slocum's registration *and* campaign. I got that much faith in him!"

The roar that went up almost deafened Slocum. He sidled away, letting Fenneman do the rhetoric. He wasn't running for sheriff. He had spent his life since the war avoiding the law, and he wasn't going to change his habits now. No one noticed him climbing into the saddle or starting out of town. He had enough information to pass along to Adam Jenks, and it wasn't good.

He felt eyes on him as he passed the fringes of the crowd. He turned and saw the Widow Clairmont watching him from the second story of Mrs. Parman's boardinghouse. She smiled, but Slocum couldn't interpret what it meant. He hoped it was as wicked as it looked, but he couldn't count on that, especially since he had no intention of returning to Van Eyck until the robbery.

Using the ends of his reins, he got his gelding moving. In minutes he was out of Van Eyck. In an hour he had found Adam Jenks's camp.

"It'll take an army to break open that bank," Slocum said, squatting down near the pot of boiling coffee. He poured more into his battered tin cup. He sipped at it without waiting for it to cool. The burning liquid tore at his mouth, but he hardly noticed. His mind was a dozen miles away, back in Van Eyck. And he wasn't sure he was thinking solely about the bank and the railroad payroll in it.

"We didn't expect it to be easy, did we, John?" asked Jenks. "Truly now, is there ever an easy robbery?"

Slocum said nothing about Jenks's change of heart about waltzing in, having the money handed to them on a silver platter, and then dashing out of Van Eyck, rich, fat, and stupid.

"We can do it. You said it might take four or five sticks of dynamite. We got that much, and we know how to use it." Jenks motioned. The one called Pecos unwrapped a blanket covering a small wooden crate. They had a dozen sticks of dynamite wrapped into a tight bundle.

"We'd have to drill into the safe to blow it. That Chubb safe is big and hard to get into."

"We know how to do it. Pecos here has done it a half dozen times. You don't drill into the door; that's no good. You drill holes into the walls around the door and blow that."

"The cage surrounding everything in the vault will be equal to the door," Slocum pointed out.

"Seldom is, truth to tell, John. I thought you knew that. Banker types enjoy putting up a heavy steel door and forgetting the sides."

Slocum remembered the steel plates and loopholes for the guards to shoot through from the lobby. He doubted Mulholland had ignored a simple thing like the walls around the vault. The brick was sturdy enough, but under it would be more steel, maybe plate, maybe bars, but it would be damned hard to get through. Still, the notion of blasting through the wall rather than the safe door seemed well reasoned and more than Slocum expected of Jenks.

"The guards just won't let you take your sweet time about drilling and blowing," Slocum said. "This bank is a fortress."

"We can plan on getting them out. They're only human, John. A woman, a drink, a few dollars, *something* will lure them away for us to do our work."

"Hitting the bank at night is the only way to do it," he said, thinking out loud. "We take a couple hours to plant the explosives, blow the wall to hell and gone, then get in." He shook his head. He didn't see how they could get through the rubble and find the payroll fast enough. The entire town was on edge because Sheriff Dawkins had hightailed it to parts unknown.

"We can do it," Jenks insisted. "We might need a bit of diversion to do it, though."

"What?" Slocum turned suspicious in a flash. The outlaw's tone told him Jenks was going to ask something Slocum didn't want to deliver. The payroll heist was still attractive to him. What man turned his back on five hundred dollars or more? But the details bogged him down. The robbery was going to be harder than finding fur on a frog.

"You said you cozied up real good to the townsfolk."

"I just ran off a pair of sneak thieves," Slocum said. "Wasn't that much to it."

"But there was, in the townsfolks' eyes." Jenks moved closer, his eyes gleaming in the firelight. He warmed his hands over the embers dying at the edge of the campfire, then turned toward Slocum. "You done something no one else in that miserable town had the nerve to do, John. To them, you are a genuine, certified hero. Truly now, why not run for sheriff?"

"You're crazy as a bedbug," Slocum declared. "I don't want to be any town's sheriff."

"No, no, listen up, John. It will work. They trust you, and you said the saloon owner was going to put up the money to get you registered for the election. What better way to find out about how they got the bank guarded?"

"Mulholland doesn't know me and wouldn't—"

"John, John, think on it a minute before sayin' no to this." Jenks rubbed his hands together as if he was ready to count all the gold coins from the robbery. "Banker Mulholland will suck up to you because you might be guardin' his bank in the future."

"March is a local. Mulholland will throw in with him. Better the devil you know than the one you don't."

Jenks snorted in contempt at such an idea. "If this March fellow is the scoundrel you make him out to be, John, don't think the town's banker hasn't decided to vote against him in favor of someone else. You're an unknown, except what you did to those two sneak thieves."

"I don't know. Mulholland might figure he can buy March. A banker having the sheriff in his hip pocket is mighty attractive. As you said, I'm an unknown. He might not want to take the chance that he can't buy me."

"What do sheriffs do, anyway? All the time they're out riding circuit and serving process. The banker knows this. He'd back you if he could pick a deputy or two from his own men."

Jenks had a good point. This would take a few guards off Mulholland's payroll and put them on the city's without taking away any of the firepower guarding his bank. Slocum had yet to see a banker who wasn't a penny-pincher intent on foreclosing on any poor wight even a few hours late on a mortgage payment. There was good reason bankers tended to be the richest citizens in any town. They took the best from the hard-working citizens, by hook or crook.

Slocum downed the last of the coffee and dropped the cup onto his bedroll. He was thinking hard of excuses to just ride on out. The payroll robbery had sounded too good to be true, and that was the way it worked out. The bank was too well guarded, the vault too thick, the building too sturdy. There were a hundred things to go wrong for every one that had to go right.

And Slocum didn't know the three men riding with Jenks. They might be all right, or they might panic if gunfire started. He remembered how they had all asked Jenks for permission to shoot when he had blundered into their camp.

Slocum would have fired first and never asked permission of any man. He seized the initiative and held on for dear life. The three riding with Jenks weren't inclined that way. And Adam Jenks wasn't a deep thinker and planning had never been his strong suit, but that didn't change the fact that the payroll would be stashed in the Bank of Van Eyck. That was a powerful draw to a man wanting enough cash to find two no-account sidewinders and get revenge on them.

Barstow and Dunphy wouldn't leave his thoughts. They had swindled him, double-crossed him, and left him for the sheriff to snare. They'd pay dearly.

But they weren't the only ones tantalizing him. Slocum couldn't get a pair of bright blue eyes out of his mind. The Widow Clairmont and the looks she had given him, both after saving Mrs. Parman and when he was riding out of town.

Maybe it wouldn't be such a bad idea going back to Van Eyck, just to nose around and see if the robbery was possible.

6

Slocum sat astride his horse and wondered what he was getting himself into. He looked north and wondered if Fort Davis might not be a better destination now, whether or not the sheriff was out hunting for him. He took a deep breath and decided not to push his luck too far. The sheriff so hot in pursuit couldn't have any idea who he was chasing, unless Barstow or Dunphy had done more than tip off the lawman to the stagecoach robbery. Although John Slocum was a wanted man, there were more notorious desperadoes riding Texas's dusty plains for any sheriff to go after.

And to the south? The road curled off into the heat-racked distance, meandering back and forth, hinting at a quick trip into Mexico across the muddy Rio Grande, then twisting back to keep a decent boundary between Texas and Mexico. That road would take him down San Antonio way, and what was wrong with that?

Slocum looked back into Van Eyck and knew. Barstow and Dunphy were out there somewhere, thinking they had gotten away scot-free. They wouldn't. He would see them both dead and drawing flies before he rode south.

Besides all this, there was the railroad payroll that soon would be pressing hard against the inner walls of the Bank of Van Eyck. He needed money, and he had to admit reluctantly that Adam Jenks had stumbled across a fine heist. There were details to be worked out, but it could be done.

He smiled slowly and let long, silky blond hair fill his thoughts. And the bluest eyes he could remember ever seeing. And the impish smile that turned more than a tad wicked. The Widow Clairmont had never said more than a few words to him, but their eyes had said more than a month of talking ever could. Slocum knew he might be dead wrong, but he didn't think he was.

"Old friend, am I getting myself into a world of trouble for a woman? Or is it just greed? That bank's mighty tempting." Slocum had trouble figuring out what drew him back to Van Eyck, but it did. He put his heels to his horse's sides and guided the animal straight down the dusty main street for the second time in two days.

He wasn't sure what to expect, but this wasn't it. The town looked deserted. He frowned, turning in the saddle as he studied the sky for the typical corroded copper whirling clouds that meant a twister was on its way. The hot sun burned his face, and there wasn't a hint of rain cloud to be seen. The people in the town had just upped and vanished, or so it seemed to him.

He rode slowly and saw people inside the buildings, most of them not even peering out. For whatever reason, the entire populace was hiding. Slocum couldn't help contrasting this to the huge crowds arguing loudly in the streets, the shouts and shoves and promises of a new sheriff in a couple weeks through election.

Dismounting, he went into Fenneman's saloon. The grizzled old man sat cross-legged at the end of the bar, a bottle of cheap whiskey on the bar beside him. Fenneman looked up and gave a broken-toothed smile when he saw Slocum.

"Knew you'd be back. There's no way you'd let me waste a gold double eagle getting you registered and what all." Fenneman tipped back the shot glass, and the murky liquor vanished down his gullet. He licked his lips, coughed, and clicked the glass to the bar. "Bad whiskey will kill you. Remember that, Slocum."

"Can't say I've decided to run for sheriff," Slocum said, wondering if there was any way around the plan Adam Jenks had formulated. "But Van Eyck's a nice enough town, and you're right about me getting footsore wandering. Might be time to spend some time rather than just passing through."

"Here. Suck on this." Fenneman pushed a half-filled glass toward Slocum. The fierce liquor burned like hell-fire.

"Potent," Slocum said, his throat burned raw from the rotgut. "Prefer the other bottle."

"Who doesn't, but it's all gone. Figured I might as well enjoy it before—"

"Before what?" Slocum asked. "It got something to do with everybody hiding away?"

"You'd make a damn fine sheriff, yes, sir." Fenneman knocked back another slug of the whiskey and made a face. Slocum had the feeling he was being set up, but couldn't decide how.

"Haven't decided," Slocum insisted, "but there might be some compensation to the job. What does it pay?"

"Not as much as it did since Dawkins made off with the town's civic development money. That don't matter much now. Not now." Fenneman stared at the clear glass of the whiskey bottle as if willing it to be full again. It stayed empty.

"You make it sound as if the whole town's dead. Didn't see many folks when I rode in, and unless I miss my guess, your saloon usually has more in it than this." Except the two of them, there wasn't a soul to be seen.

"Heard tell there's a passel of outlaws on the way to town. Nobody's going to stand up against 'em."

"So?" Slocum didn't understand what was going on. "What do a few owlhoots have to do with the hangdog look to Van Eyck?"

"They're gonna rob the bank!" The words exploded from the scraggly-bearded saloon owner. "They rob that danged bank and the railroad will pull out of Van Eyck entirely. This whole place will shrivel up and die. The railroad money's all we got keeping us going."

Slocum didn't want to point out that the railroad already had bypassed the town and that meant they were doomed

to become just another ghost town soon. The payroll from
the railroad might be keeping Van Eyck alive now, but
the townspeople would evaporate like spit in the burning
desert sun when the construction moved on down the line.
The best the citizens of Van Eyck could hope for was
postponing, not preventing, their town's demise.

"They're going to rob the bank?" Coldness welled inside
him when he thought it through. If another gang robbed the
bank, that meant Slocum and Jenks's gang would be left
twisting in the wind.

"That's the rumor. Without a decent sheriff, there's nothing to stop them. And I don't see March doing much in the
way of planning to run off any robbers."

"That bank's a fortress. I put money into it. Banker
Mulholland has a young army swarming all over the place.
A sheriff and an entire posse's not going to match the
firepower aimed at anybody trying to steal from the Bank
of Van Eyck."

"He lost some of his guards. Mulholland's fuming mad
about it, but he wasn't paying spit. Half dozen walked out
on him. He's probably got the tellers cowering behind their
cages with scatterguns."

"They're more likely to shoot each other," Slocum said.

"The real irony of it is, there ain't much in the vault right
now. The big payroll's not due for another week."

"Any gang worth its salt would know that," Slocum
said.

"We're talking about the New Braunfals Bunch. They
don't care as much for money as they do killin'. You've
seen their like, Slocum. I can read it in your eyes." Fenneman ran his finger around the rim of his shot glass, found
nothing damp, and jumped to the floor. He rummaged
around behind the bar but didn't come up with another
bottle. Shrugging, he just leaned. The bar was closed, empty
of liquor.

"I've seen men like that," Slocum said, remembering the
utter glee men like Bloody Bill Anderson took in murdering
helpless women and children. War was hell and that was
about all that bastard Sherman had ever said that was true,

but wanton killing wasn't the way to win. It only made for resentment that burned for years in the survivors.

"The railroad's likely to either keep their money or put it in some other town's bank if Mulholland gets robbed."

"On the other hand, if this New Braunfals Bunch is run off, the railroad's more inclined to store their payroll in Van Eyck," Slocum finished for him. His mind raced. It would be a godsend if the railroad kept the payroll; it would be easier to pry loose from an armored railcar than Mulholland's bank. But the payroll might also be put in some other bank. That meant Slocum would have to start his planning over again. The Bank of Van Eyck was a tough nut to crack, but Slocum had a few ideas how to approach it. A new bank meant new problems—and probably a town with a sheriff. It might even be the sheriff who had pursued him so eagerly after the stagecoach robbery.

"What's on your mind, Slocum? You're cogitatin' awful hard." Fenneman cocked his head to one side and smiled crookedly.

"Is March up to defending the bank? I'm thinking a few of us with rifles on the rooftops might discourage any robbers."

Fenneman snorted in contempt at the notion of March doing anything resembling a sheriff's work. "That no-account just wants the graft that goes with being sheriff. He saw how much Dawkins made off with and thinks he can do the same. He wouldn't risk his hide if his own granny was in trouble."

"Deputize a posse?" Slocum suggested.

Again Fenneman snorted in disgust. "The town's better at arguing than doing. Mulholland's trying like fury to get more guards, but he's not having much luck. Not at what he's offering. And there's no way of deputizing if the town doesn't have a sheriff."

"Mulholland might offer more to run off the road agents," Slocum said. Fenneman didn't have to answer for Slocum to see that Mulholland was, indeed, like all the other bankers. He'd let thieves steal everything in his bank, down to the last brick, before he'd open his fist to let out a few pennies.

"Vigilance committee to protect the town?" Slocum suggested. Fenneman didn't even offer his opinion on this. Van Eyck had turned too complacent and the citizens figured the law ought to protect them. They didn't understand— or remember—that the best law often rested in their own hands and guns.

"Reckon this means you're going to ride on out of town. After you get your money out of Mulholland's bank."

"It was only ten dollars," Slocum said, thinking hard about the ways he could turn this to his benefit. He needed the money from the bank. "Anybody ever see this New Braunfals Bunch? Know what they look like?"

"There might be a poster on them over at the sheriff's office, but Dawkins wasn't much for keeping loose paper. He wasn't much at doing anything, now that I ponder on it."

Slocum left without another word, going straight for the deserted sheriff's office. He rummaged through the sheriff's desk, looking for any wanted posters on the New Braunfals Bunch, but he didn't find anything. He rocked back in the sheriff's chair, trying to remember if he'd ever heard of them. He hadn't, and that struck him as strange.

Turning back to the scattered posters, Slocum went through them more carefully, looking for his own face on one. He breathed a sigh of relief when he didn't find it. A sudden noise at the door made him grab for his Colt. He had the six-shooter out and aimed before he realized the Widow Clairmont was standing there, staring at him with her incredibly lovely azure eyes.

"Mr. Slocum, Fenneman said you were over here."

"How'd he know where I was going? I didn't tell him."

"Why, I assume he watched as you left his establishment," she said, brushing back a strand of silken blond hair. She tucked it demurely under her gingham bonnet. "I wanted to talk to you. We've never been properly introduced, and I know this isn't proper." She straightened her skirts, took in a deep breath that focused Slocum's attention squarely on her, then said, "My name is Samantha

Clairmont, and I think it is wonderful what you did for
Mrs. Parman."

"Wasn't anything special," Slocum said, watching the
rise and fall of the woman's breasts under her tight bodice.
He couldn't remember ever seeing a lovelier woman.

"Oh, but it was. You are a hero."

"Don't feel very heroic right now. Fenneman wants me
to run for sheriff and—"

"That's why I wanted to speak with you. May I, sir?"
She indicted a dilapidated chair. Slocum didn't care what
she did as long as she didn't leave.

"Thank you," she said, folding her hands primly in her
lap. Slocum looked at those delicate hands and thought
something didn't seem right. Something wasn't right with
them, but his attention shifted when she took another deep
breath.

"I have formed a ladies' committee to elect you sheriff
of Van Eyck, if you will run. I know you're not a citizen,
but we feel you are the man for the job."

"You don't know anything about me."

"That it is you sitting in that chair doing the sheriff's
work rather than Mr. March tells me all I need to know.
And Mr. March was present when those ruffians beset Mrs.
Parman. He did nothing. You acted without consideration
for your personal safety."

"I was trying to get a handle on the New Braunfals
Bunch," Slocum said. "Can't seem to find anything about
them. No wanted posters, nothing."

Samantha Clairmont frowned, and Slocum thought she
was even lovelier the way her nose wrinkled slightly. "I
had not heard of them, either, until Mr. March described
the horrors they have perpetrated elsewhere. They are from
East Texas, I believe."

"March has been telling everyone the outlaws are coming?"

"Why, not just him. Others. Everyone knows."

Slocum knew how rumors were started and how they
spread like a prairie fire. He'd bet the ten dollars he'd put
in Mulholland's bank who had started the rumor about a

vicious gang heading toward Van Eyck.

"Well, Mrs. Clairmont, I'm sure everyone does know."

"It is a terrible time to beseech you to be our sheriff, but I must. You are the type of man who can save us, brave, strong—" She smiled. Slocum returned it.

"Before I declare for sheriff, let's see what I can do about this New Braunfals Bunch."

"If anyone can save us, I'm sure you are the one, Mr. Slocum." She reached over and lightly touched his hand. Then she was gone, a mirage of beauty in the desolate town of Van Eyck.

Slocum heaved a sigh, got a faint hint of her perfume, and then left the office. He had work to do.

7

Slocum checked his rifle a second time. He wanted to be sure nothing went wrong when the New Braunfals Bunch rode into town. He walked along slowly, stopping for a moment in front of Mrs. Parman's white clapboard boardinghouse. Down the street, March harangued a small group of citizens, declaring he was the only native choice for sheriff, that Slocum was an interloper, that he had evil intentions for Van Eyck.

"If he only knew," Slocum said under his breath. He turned at small movement dimly seen from the corner of his eye. The curtains on the second-floor front window moved slightly. He saw Samantha Clairmont staring at him. He smiled and tipped his hat in her direction, and she favored him with a broad grin.

Then all hell broke loose in Van Eyck.

Masked men thundered into town, shooting out windows and scaring horses tethered along the streets. Most of the townspeople were indoors, as much for protection from the hot sun as fear of the very group of outlaws heading straight for the bank.

"It's the New Braunfals Bunch!" someone shouted. The small crowd around March vanished, leaving the portly candidate on his soapbox, jaw open, but no sounds coming from his mouth. His eyes widened in surprise, then turned to outright fear.

"Kill 'em," one of the outlaws shouted. "Kill the whole damn town!" Bullets flew and windows broke. Women shrieked, and the men of the town dived for cover. They weren't going up against the orneriest, most dangerous band of highwaymen to leave East Texas. They had heard the tall tales and weren't willing to stick around to see the reality.

"There's the bank. Take it, men!" ordered the masked leader. "Don't leave anybody alive inside!"

Slocum began firing his Winchester with great deliberation. One outlaw's six-shooter went flying from his hand. Another grabbed at his side and doubled over, moaning loudly.

"There's only the one of 'em," the leader said, wheeling his horse around. "Take him out!"

Slocum's rifle came up empty. He whipped out his Colt and fired three times. A second would-be robber shuddered and almost fell from the saddle. He managed to grab hold of his saddle horn and guide his horse toward the edge of town. Slocum rushed forward, dodging bullets as he ran. He got close enough to the leader to level his six-shooter at his gut.

"Give up. Surrender or die!"

"Like hell! The New Braunfals Bunch don't surrender to no tin-badged lawman!"

Slocum fired point-blank. The outlaw recoiled and stared at his shirt. In the center of a ring of unburned powder blazed a tiny spark from the wadding. The outlaw's shirt caught fire; he roared like a stepped-on grizzly and kicked his horse to motion.

"Get out of here. Run, boys. The law's too tough in this town. Truly they are!"

Slocum watched the last of the New Braunfals Bunch retreat. Van Eyck was safe for a while longer. He fired the last rounds in his Colt at their backs, then ran for his horse.

"Slocum, you fool, what are you doing?" called Fenneman from just inside his saloon.

"Going after them. They were the New Braunfals Bunch you were worrying about. You don't want them coming back for revenge, do you?"

"Take some men with you. You can't handle them alone."

"Where's March? If he'll ride with me, we can take them together. He knows all about their ways." Slocum saw a tight knot of men edging from an alleyway where they'd watched the brief skirmish with the New Braunfals Bunch. His words weren't lost on them.

"March hightailed it when the shooting started," one man said. "Don't rightly know where he got off to."

"Then it's up to me." Slocum wheeled his gelding around and took off after the fleeing road agents. He galloped until he was out of town, then slowed to keep from tiring his horse. He didn't know how far he'd have to ride. As it turned out, when he topped a rise, he found the four outlaws waiting for him.

"Dammit, Slocum, you didn't have to go and set fire to me like that," complained Adam Jenks. He had stripped off his shirt and had stamped out the fire.

"When we hit the bank and get the payroll, you'll be able to buy a hundred new shirts," Slocum said. "The rest of you all right? Nobody from town took a potshot at you?"

"They all hid like rabbits," Jenks said, speaking for his men. He started laughing until tears came to his eyes. "Reckon this gets you elected sheriff, don't it?"

Slocum said nothing. The entire charade had been played out well enough. If anyone stopped to wonder, they might doubt a single man's ability to chase off a band of determined, vicious outlaws. But he didn't think anyone in Van Eyck would make the effort. He had asked Jenks about the New Braunfals Bunch and had gotten the same vacant-eyed recognition—or lack of it.

If anyone would know of another company of bandits operating in West Texas, it'd be Jenks. None of them had ever heard of the New Braunfals Bunch. That meant the outlaws were March's creation. Whip up a little fear and March would be a shoo-in for sheriff. The mock raid had been worth the risk, just to see March's expression when his phantoms turned real. More than that, Slocum knew he had nothing more to worry about in casing the bank. The guards were gone and Mulholland would see him as the best way of protecting the railroad's payroll.

"Fox in charge of the henhouse," Slocum muttered.

"How's that, John? We truly did well this day, don't you think?"

"You get on back to camp," Slocum said. "I'll let you know when the payroll comes into town. Prying it loose from the bank is looking easier by the minute."

"You do that now, old son. Me and the boys will be waiting for your signal. Then we're all going to be rich!"

Slocum rode slowly back to Van Eyck, working up a story that would put him in the best light. It wasn't hard. After all, hadn't he singlehandedly driven off the dreaded New Braunfals Bunch?

"Where was Mr. March? Nowhere to be seen, that's where!" declared Samantha Clairmont with conviction. "There is no one better suited to be our next sheriff than Mr. John Slocum!"

Slocum tried not to mind the cheer that went up. Such adulation could go to a man's head mighty fast, and if the people of Van Eyck ever found out he had staged the robbery, their mood would quickly change. He touched his neck where sweat beaded next to the bandanna. He'd be worrying about rope burns if March got wind of the deception.

He saw his opponent at the edge of the crowd. March looked fit to be tied. He had invented the New Braunfals Bunch to scare the town, and the lie had turned around and bitten him in the butt like a stepped-on sidewinder.

"Mr. Slocum, a few words, please." Samantha gave him one of her radiant smiles. He rose and held up his hand to still the cheer rising from the gathering.

"I'm not much for speechifying."

"Unlike someone else we all know," a wit in the crowd called loudly. All eyes turned to March, who flushed furiously and spun to hurry off. Laughter followed his footsteps.

"I'm not saying March is a coward," Slocum said, trying to put himself into the best light without going overboard, "but he made himself mighty scarce when you needed him. I'm not a hero. I just happened to be at the right spot to do you some service."

He sat down quickly, amid more cheers. If the election had been held then and there, he'd've received every vote in town, maybe even March's.

"Please come to the dance tonight," Samantha said in a clear voice that carried over the crowd noise. "We'll celebrate."

The crowd dispersed. Slocum sat and watched, wondering what to do now. Fenneman had run dry at the town's only saloon. He'd promised to mix up more whiskey as soon as the grain alcohol arrived, but that might be days. Slocum felt his throat tightening at the notion of making all these speeches without some liquid fortifier.

"Mr. Slocum, please do me the honor of joining me for tea." Samantha Clairmont stared at him with those guileless blue eyes. He couldn't refuse her.

"Be honored, Mrs. Clairmont," he said.

"Please, call me Samantha." She averted her eyes demurely and said, "And may I call you John?"

"Nothing could please me more," Slocum said.

"Indeed." This time she stared quite boldly into his green eyes. He saw the devil dancing in hers and suddenly didn't dread the notion of tea in Mrs. Parman's front parlor at all.

They walked to the boardinghouse and went inside. Slocum looked around. The rooms were neat and clean, if a bit threadbare. The furniture was worn and holes in the carpeting had patches on patches. A well-polished narrow wood staircase led to the upstairs bedrooms.

"Where's Mrs. Parman?" he asked.

"Away for the afternoon." Samantha turned, her face upturned and just inches away. "Do you really want tea?"

Slocum hesitated. He didn't much like tea, and he'd never trade it for what he thought this lovely woman offered. But she was so modest, so decorous—

The way she kissed him combined passion and need in a mixture that set him on fire. Samantha moved even closer for a second kiss, her body pressing boldly against his. He felt the tight, firm breasts crushing against his chest, her hips grinding into his, and the woman's strong hands holding his head firmly in place for the kiss. When her tongue sneaked out and toyed with his, he knew he didn't have to worry about being polite over afternoon tea.

His hands moved around her lithe body and pulled her even closer. His left hand slid across the small of her back while his right cupped firm buttocks. Samantha lifted one leg and hooked it around his back. There was only one way for them to be even closer.

"Where?" he gasped out. "Here?"

Samantha laughed in delight. "What a wonderful idea, John," she said, "but we'd better go upstairs to my bedroom. It's the one at—"

"I can find it," he said, stifling her answer with another kiss. He swung her off her feet and carried the clinging woman up the stairs. She kept one long leg curled around his back and the other locked behind his right leg. She seemed as light as a feather as he came to the door, but he fumbled at the cut-glass doorknob.

"Let me," she said, reaching around him to open the door. Somehow, she managed to excite him even more with the movement. She bobbed up and down slightly, rubbing her loins against his. And her hand stroked over his back and neck. Slocum spun into the room and dropped her on the feather bed. Samantha rocked back and bounced, ending up in a lewd position. Her legs were up and her skirt hiked past her waist. Slocum saw she wasn't wearing anything under her many skirts.

"It's hot, John," she said. He didn't know if she was talking about the weather or something else, but he would find out. He dropped his gun belt and kicked out of his boots. Samantha hurried to help him with the buttons on his pants. Somehow, her fingers stroking and probing made it harder for him to get free of his unwanted clothing. Samantha only laughed delightedly at his predicament.

He finally stepped out of his trousers. Samantha whirled on the bed, her fingers wrapping around the hardness she found growing at his groin. "So tasty looking," she said. She licked it slowly, her rough tongue starting at the base and working up.

Slocum laced his fingers through her lustrous blond hair and pulled her back. "Don't," he said. "That feels mighty fine, but it's been so long."

"A handsome, strong man like you?" she teased. "I can hardly believe it." She continued to stroke and tease until Slocum felt as if his boiler was going to burst. He pushed her flat on the bed and dropped down between her wantonly spread thighs.

"This is what I really want," he said.

"Then take it, John. I'm yours. All yours." She pulled his head back down and kissed him hard. He moved forward, the tip of his manhood brushing against her lust-dampened nether lips. Samantha groaned softly and threw her head back over the edge of the bed. Shudders of rapt anticipation raced through her.

"I need you, John. Don't deny me now. Take me, take me hard!"

She arched her back and slammed down around his length so hard that it took Slocum's breath away. Her hips moved in quick little circles, then began a more powerful grinding motion when she had taken him fully into her heated interior.

It was time for Slocum to take the initiative. Up to this point, the blond had been doing everything. His hands slipped under her round, hard buttocks and he lifted her up to just the right position. He started sliding back and forth, slowly at first, then with greater speed and penetration. She thrashed about, moaning constantly now. Slocum was unrelenting in his movements, driving deep, pausing, and then slowly retreating. Every gyration only added to their enjoyment.

He felt the white-hot tide rising within him much too soon. He wanted this lovemaking to last, to enjoy it to the fullest, but it had been so long since he'd been with a woman. His body rode on faster than his mind.

"Go on, John, now, do it now. Oh! *Oh!*"

She threw her arms high over her head, shoving her hips down onto his fleshy stalk. Slocum felt tight inner muscles clamp down firmly on his hidden length and knew there was no more time for him. He began stroking rapidly now, trying to split her apart with every stroke. The tides rose within him and he couldn't hold back. He exploded, her clinging female tunnel milking him for every drop locked in his balls.

They clung to one another, rolling over and over on the bed until there wasn't anything left. Slocum sagged weakly to the featherbed, Samantha's face just inches from his.

"You make love as good as you save towns," she said.

"One was just luck," he said.

"Let's find out which one," Samantha said, her fingers already teasing his manhood again. It took a spell to get hard again, but Slocum wasn't complaining. And neither was Samantha Clairmont.

8

"They swallowed it, hook, line, and sinker," chortled Adam Jenks. He rubbed his hands together. "Truly, John, this is the finest moment of my life. We will have that entire payroll handed to us as sweet as you please."

Slocum grew increasingly uneasy at the way Jenks thought of the robbery as nothing more than a church's Sunday social. It wasn't going to be easy. Mulholland had managed to hire two men to stand guard. That didn't worry Slocum as much as the notion the railroad might post men of their own around town. The Irish steel drivers could fell a bull with a single blow. Slocum had watched two of them having at each other in a bare-knuckles fistfight. No human could possibly take the punishment meted out in that fight, yet both had.

And they had even smiled through the blood and broken teeth, the best of friends. Men like this weren't trifled with.

"There'll be a few minutes getting into the vault that'll be the most dangerous," Slocum said. "The explosion might bring the town running. We have to be ready, if it does."

"That's rich, Slocum. *You're* the sheriff. You'll be the one doing the running. They trust you. Just tell 'em to back off, and they will." Jenks laughed again, then added, "Hell, ask them to help us load the greenbacks onto a pack mule. They *trust* you."

Slocum's mind drifted as Jenks and the others started lying to one another about how they'd spend their part of the take. He had heard dozens of men weaving these dreams and knew that few of them were real. One of Jenks's men—Ed—wanted to buy a few acres and start a ranch. He'd lose the money in a crooked card game. The others' reasons for wanting the money weren't any better. They'd piss the money away on loose women and hard liquor.

He just couldn't get Samantha Clairmont out of his mind. Something about her bothered him. The contradiction of being so demure in public and such a wanton when they were alone wasn't it. He had seen enough women throw off the shackles of what society expected of them to appreciate her passion.

Something else bothered him. He scratched himself, remembering the feel of Samantha's mouth moving in the same area. And her hands. He frowned. There was something about her hands.

"John, I say, John. Are you still with us? You want to play a few hands of poker before going back to your town?"

"It's not my town, and I got to be moving on," Slocum said, rising. He had no reason to play cards with Jenks's men. He never played for fun; if there wasn't money to be had, why bother? If he cleaned the lot of them out, he would hardly have enough to buy himself a bottle of Fenneman's vile rotgut whiskey.

"Sure it's just devotion to looking after our payroll?" asked Jenks. Slocum turned and stared at the man.

"What do you mean by that?" he asked coldly. He wasn't going to take anything off Jenks, not now.

"Why, John, truly I don't mean a thing. It's just that there's a lingering odor about you that wasn't there before."

"Perfume," Johnny said, making it sound like an indictment.

"Yes, sir, it surely does smell like you've got perfume on. Or maybe it just rubbed off, eh?" Jenks laughed and the others joined in. Slocum smiled, but there wasn't any humor in it. He rode straight back to Van Eyck.

"Evening, Sheriff Slocum," a man walking along the board-walk said. Slocum recoiled, startled at the sound of his name coupled with the title of sheriff. "Reckon we'll see you at the meeting later."

"What meeting's that?" he asked, to cover his confusion. Sheriff Slocum sounded wrong to him. He didn't like it. Not one bit.

"Why, there's a rally this evening to call out all the citizens to support your election," came the answer.

"Don't remember agreeing to anything like that," Slocum said.

"That Mrs. Clairmont is a real caution. She's doing the work of a man turning out the voters. One day, women will have the vote, then, mark my words, look out." The man was silenced by loud guffaws from his two friends. The trio turned into Fenneman's saloon, leaving Slocum behind on the boardwalk.

Slocum wished that Samantha wouldn't go to such lengths in his behalf. He had no intention of being elected sheriff, much less pinning the badge on and serving as such. Leaving the town in March's hands wasn't too much of a crime, Slocum thought, not with Van Eyck getting ready to turn into a ghost town. The railroad crews would move on to the end of the line, the payroll money would evaporate, and other towns would spring up along the tracks.

As he walked, Slocum wondered how far away the railroad tracks were. He didn't remember anyone saying, and the crews didn't make it in to town to drink Fenneman's whiskey. The railroad bosses might be smarter than he gave them credit for. Putting the tracks off in the middle of the desert kept their crews sober enough, except for a once-a-month blow-off in a nearby town.

Had the crews ever come into Van Eyck and torn it up? A few fights among the handful of railroad men he'd seen didn't count. A full company of Irish track layers would drink like there was no tomorrow and fight like there was. Keeping the peace on that night would be nothing short of hell on earth.

Slocum shook himself. He was starting to think like a sheriff. What did he care if the railroad crews burned Van Eyck to the ground? All he wanted from the town was easy entry into Mulholland's bank when the time was right.

He walked toward the dark hulk of the bank and just stared at it. Blowing a hole through the side might be a quick way in, but it also would cause unwanted attention. Better to get into the lobby, then work on the vault out of sight. That would give them several extra minutes to work after the dynamite went off, if anyone even heard the blast. Slocum smiled slightly at the notion that he might even be given keys to the bank. He could tell Mulholland he saw strangers nosing around and needed to get in quietly to see what they were up to.

This robbery was looking better to him by the minute. With even a little luck, he'd have more than enough money to keep him in food and his gelding in grain for months. Slocum turned and started away from the bank, not wanting to seem too attentive. People might get the wrong idea—or the right one—about his intentions.

At the far end of the street, torches had been driven into the ground. Thick clouds of black smoke billowed and obscured what was happening. A vagrant night breeze off the desert blew the cloud away and Slocum saw March setting up a podium. He remembered reading a broadside about this being a big get-together, complete with food and beer. Slocum wondered if Samantha planned to compete with free food or if she'd have the rally afterward.

Slocum just hoped he wouldn't be forced to make another speech. It was easier sitting on a horse, hands tied behind his back, waiting for the noose to tighten than facing dozens of eager, honest people and lying to them.

He turned toward the saloon when he heard a fight start inside. He wanted to keep on walking. The new whiskey Fenneman had cooked up was a killer, strong enough to eat the bluing off a pistol barrel. Any man drinking it would go blind and crazy, and not necessarily in that order.

Slocum shook himself again. There he was, thinking like a sheriff. This was useful at times, after he'd robbed a train or bank and needed to know what the law might do. But now? He had no call thinking like a lawman, much less *acting* like one.

"John, there you are. Come quickly. Please!" Samantha Clairmont rushed out of the shadows cast by the general store and grabbed his arm with a strong grip.

"Evening," he said, looking around to see if anyone was watching. If they'd been alone, he'd've shown Samantha how glad he was to see her again. Three other women stood a few paces back, so he couldn't do more than be polite. But later—

"We were on our way to the rally when it—he—oh, I don't know what to say." She looked distraught enough to confuse even the simplest of things. Slocum looked uneasily from Samantha to the women with her. He didn't want her revealing how they'd spent the afternoon while Mrs. Parman was out. It could only harm Samantha's reputation in town and draw suspicion to Slocum. He wanted to appear lily-white until the robbery. Then his reputation wouldn't matter.

But what then of Samantha's? Slocum forced himself to ignore that.

"Tell him, dear. Just come right out and tell Mr. Slocum," advised a woman with Samantha.

"Did the two come back to town?" Slocum asked, wondering what could be upsetting Samantha so much.

"No, not them. Another one. Worse. Worse even than any of the New Braunfals Bunch."

Slocum looked at her sharply. Something in Samantha's tone was mocking but at the same time imploring. It was as if she laughed at some joke and yet was deadly serious. Slocum couldn't make head nor tail of her attitude.

"There's a man in Fenneman's saloon intent on killing everyone in sight. I am sure of it," Samantha said forthrightly. "If he is not stopped quickly, he will certainly murder someone. He is drunk and disorderly and—"

"Whoa, hold your horses, Mrs. Clairmont," said Slocum. "I don't have any authority to stop any drunkard from shooting up the place. The election's not for a couple weeks. I'm just a candidate running for sheriff."

"You stopped those thugs brutalizing Mrs. Parman," Samantha said. "And don't forget how you saved us all

by routing the New Braunfals Bunch." Again he heard a
note of mockery in her voice. He wondered if she had
figured out that he hadn't risked a damned thing chasing
off Jenks and his men, that it had been entirely staged.

"Why not let March show his mettle by taking care of
this?" he asked. "If he's running for sheriff, too, he ought
to get an equal chance to prove himself."

"Mr. March," another woman informed him coldly, "told
us to mind our own busine;s."

"John, please. This is serious. I know when a man is
intent on killing. This one is so drunk—" Samantha bit off
her words, as if she was saying too much. She looked up
at him, blue eyes as big as saucers. "Please."

He couldn't refuse her when she looked at him that way
and spoke with such urgency. Slocum damned himself for
a complete fool, slipped the leather thong off the hammer of
his Colt, and went to Fenneman's saloon to find the trouble-
maker who was getting Samantha and the other ladies so
riled up. Pausing for a moment to let his eyes adjust to the
bright light inside, he sensed the tension in the large room.
Samantha pressed close behind him, peering around.

"Fenneman's cowed," she said in a husky whisper. "See
him behind the bar?"

"You ladies wait down the street a few rods," Slocum
said. He didn't want Samantha getting in the line of fire.
Fenneman was the least of the problem in the large room.
The saloon's owner stood pasty-faced, his back pressed
against the wall as if someone had lined him up to be shot.

Others in the room had similar expressions on their faces.
They were waiting for someone to die, and they were all
afraid it might be them.

The source of the commotion was a bandy-legged man
with his back to the door. He had a six-shooter drawn
and was waving it around. As Slocum watched, the man
squeezed off a round that shattered the mirror behind the
bar. Fenneman flinched but didn't duck to avoid a second shot.

"That's good, old man, real good. You keep followin'
my advice about tryin' to disappear and you might walk

out of here alive. Then again, maybe not. Maybe none of you will leave here alive. I'm in a killing mood tonight."

Slocum drew his Colt and walked forward on cat's feet. He came within two paces of the man before a floorboard squeaked and gave him away. As he swung around to face Slocum, his face blossomed into surprise and fear.

Slocum didn't give Dunphy an instant's quarter. He swung his pistol as hard as he could, laying the barrel alongside the man's head. The sick crunch told of metal smashing bone. Dunphy dropped as if he had been poleaxed. Slocum stood over his former partner and just stared at him. His trigger finger twitched. It would be easy to get his revenge. All he had to do was lift the Navy Colt a mite and pull the hair trigger. The slug would rip out Dunphy's vile life once and for all.

"You can't just go and kill him, Slocum," came Fenneman's aggrieved voice. "He's got to pay for what he done."

"He'll pay," Slocum said. "He'll pay plenty."

Dunphy's eyes flickered. In spite of the mighty bashing he had endured, he was coming around. Slocum figured it meant Dunphy's head was even thicker than he'd thought. Double-crossing him wasn't the act of a bright man, but taking a gun barrel like he had and being able to even move meant his skull was made of solid bone.

"Slocum, don't," Dunphy started. Slocum moved like a striking snake, his boot kicking out and catching the man's gun hand. Dunphy's six-gun flew from his grip.

"Give me a reason to cut you down, you son of a bitch," Slocum said, cocking his Colt and pointing it squarely between Dunphy's fear-widened eyes.

"Don't kill me." Dunphy was starting to realize what a fix he was in. He broke into a sweat and was going to start begging. Slocum's finger tightened on the trigger. It wouldn't take much to keep the stagecoach robbery secret from everyone in Van Eyck.

Just a fraction of an inch before the trigger released the Colt's hammer, Slocum relaxed. He wanted Dunphy dead, but he also wanted to find Barstow and get his share of the money from the stage robbery. By his reckoning, his share now amounted to the entire take. They shouldn't have crossed him.

"Take him on over to the jail, Slocum," Fenneman said. "That's the only fair thing. Let him sleep off his drunk. He was just feelin' a mite frisky. Didn't harm nobody."

"That's right. I didn't hurt none of 'em," pleaded Dunphy.

Slocum chanced a look over his shoulder and saw Samantha and her friends watching him. He ought to put Dunphy out of his miserable existence, but he couldn't. Not with everyone watching. And he had to ask a few questions that were better answered in private.

"Get moving," Slocum said, grabbing Dunphy's collar and pulling him erect. "I'm taking you to jail."

Slocum pushed past the men gathered around and then crowded past the tight knot of women standing in the saloon's doorway. Samantha smiled brightly and blew him a kiss that no one else saw. Slocum had no time for her, not with Dunphy walking a few paces ahead of a gun's muzzle.

"Slocum, thanks for getting me out of there. Where are we going?"

"The jail's right here, Dunphy." Slocum shoved his former partner into the small office. "I ought to put a bullet in your gut and watch you die. You set that sheriff on my trail."

"No, no, you got it all wrong. We didn't know Sheriff Tallant was going to be out there."

"You know his name? What'd you and Barstow do, tip him off before the robbery, then find a place to hole up while Tallant chased me to the ends of the earth?" Slocum saw the man's reaction and knew he'd hit the nail square on the head.

"No, it wasn't like that, Slocum. It was all Barstow's doing. He made me do it. We been trail mates for quite a spell. I couldn't go against him, not even for you."

"It didn't take much convincing, if I'm any judge."

Dunphy blinked, then a small smile crept to the corners of his mouth. "You ain't no judge, Slocum, but it looks like they think you're a lawman. How'd that happen?" Dunphy looked around the sheriff's office as if looking for something to steal. Slocum swung his pistol and dropped Dunphy to his knees with another blow to the head. He didn't want the outlaw shooting off his mouth in public about the short time they'd ridden together.

Slocum grabbed Dunphy's collar and dragged him back to the two cells in the back room. Slocum wasn't in the mood to drag Dunphy too far; he dropped him in the first cell and slammed the door shut just as the man stirred and rubbed the side of his head.

"You didn't have no call doing that, Slocum. I'm square with you on this. Barstow's the man you want. He's got all the money."

Slocum pulled out a small roll of greenbacks from Dunphy's shirt pocket and held them up.

"You didn't have two nickels to rub together before the robbery. Now you've got almost fifty dollars. If it didn't come from the stagecoach's strongbox, then where? Your sainted maiden aunt?"

Before Dunphy could lie about the money, Slocum heard a commotion in the office. He ducked out of the room and back into the office. Samantha and her friends had crowded into the small room.

"Mr. Slocum," Samantha said with stiff formality, "what do you intend doing with that miscreant?"

It took Slocum a second to understand what she meant. He said, "I'll keep him locked up till he sobers, then ride him out of town." What Slocum would actually do with the outlaw once they'd gotten outside Van Eyck was something else. He knew a half dozen Apache tortures that no man could resist. He'd find out where the rest of the money from the stage robbery was—and where Barstow was hiding.

"We just wanted to be sure," Samantha said, relaxing a little. "We were afraid you might mistreat your prisoner. After all, you did deal him quite a vicious blow."

"But it was deserved," a woman chimed in. "We saw what he was doing, and you handled it well, Mr. Slocum."

"Everything's under control, ladies. Why don't you—"

The loud report from a rifle almost deafened Slocum. He spun, hand on his six-shooter, but he didn't draw. He hadn't been the target, but he knew who had. He kicked open the door to the cells and saw Dunphy sprawled on the floor, a pool of blood forming under him. The single round had come through the window and taken off the top of his head.

9

Slocum unlocked the heavy iron cell door and stepped over Dunphy's still body, careful not to get blood on his boots. He cautiously peered out the barred window but saw nothing. The night was dark, and Dunphy's killer could be standing just a few feet off and Slocum would never spot him.

But he knew who had pulled the trigger. Who else but Barstow had any call to kill Dunphy?

"This is horrible," Samantha said, staring at the body on the jail floor. One of her friends had fainted and the other two tried not to look distressed. From their white, pinched faces Slocum knew they hadn't seen death before. He slid his Colt out and checked it. The night had suddenly turned very dangerous.

"You stay here," Slocum ordered. "I'll see if I can find who did this."

"John," Samantha said, clinging to his arm with her strong hand, "be careful. I don't want anything to happen to you."

He looked into her blue eyes and knew she meant it. He touched her hand, then moved away quickly. If he wanted to get Barstow before he left town, he'd have to hurry. Slocum hurried around the jail, Colt Navy going in front of him. The muzzle turned into a hunting dog, restlessly moving in the night, seeking a target—and not finding it. Slocum spent ten minutes searching for any sign of Barstow and couldn't find anything. He gave up in disgust and returned to the jail's small office.

The women with Samantha had left, but she sat primly in the straight-backed wood chair, her hands folded in her lap. Fenneman and two others Slocum had seen lounging around town crowded into the office, waiting for him to tell them of his success.

"Any luck, Mr. Slocum?" asked Samantha.

He shook his head. "Got clean away." He looked from face to face and puzzled over the differences. Fenneman looked almost eager. The stout man with the handlebar mustache looked scared as hell. The man with him was only a toady, worried more about what his boss thought than anything else. And Samantha was composed, not like the other women who had gone to pieces at the sight of sudden, bloody death. She seemed to accept it like a man.

"Do you have any idea who might have slain that poor unfortunate?" she asked.

He caught a note of mockery in her words, as if she was toying with him again. How could she know he, Dunphy, and Barstow had tried to rob the coach? There wasn't any way, he decided. It was just her way of talking. He had seen it before when she'd mentioned the New Braunfals Bunch, and there wasn't any cause for him to get worried about it.

"He was just another citizen," Slocum said. "I don't know many folks here in Van Eyck." He looked at the stout man, who twirled his mustaches nervously.

"He was just a drifter come to town," Fenneman said. Slocum kept watching the heavy-set man, wondering why he was here. Fenneman took a delight in anything that brought adventure to his dull life. He would certainly rejoice that Dunphy had gotten his head blown off for all the outlaw had done to the saloon keeper earlier.

"Not much anyone can do, then. I searched him and there's no way of identifying him." Slocum didn't mention the fifty dollars riding high in his shirt pocket he'd taken off Dunphy. It was little enough pay for what he was going through. His only regret was that he hadn't ended the miserable snake's life himself.

That made killing Barstow all the sweeter, though.

"We, uh, we haven't met formally, Mr. Slocum. I am George Leroy."

"He's mayor of Van Eyck," chimed in his fleshy shadow, looking adoringly at his boss.

"Shut up, Jed. I *am* mayor and congratulate you on your decision to run for sheriff. However, there seems to be growing violence in our streets."

"This ugly murder," said Jed.

"And the New Braunfals Bunch riding into town the way they did," cut in Samantha, smiling slightly. She studied Slocum as if he were a bug under a magnifying glass, and she was waiting to see which way he would squirm.

"The trend toward violence in what had once been a peaceful town is deplorable," Mayor Leroy went on, as if he hadn't been interrupted. "Something must be done about it."

"The election's not far off. You'll have yourself an elected sheriff after it that most of the townsfolk want," Slocum said, uneasy at the way things were going. He wanted to rob the bank, not be their damned sheriff.

"We realize that, but ever since Sheriff Dawkins took his extended leave of absence—"

"The bastard stole our money, George. Come on out and admit it," interrupted Fenneman, obviously enjoying this to the hilt. "Just go on and ask Slocum. He knows what's been going on here. Go on."

"Yes, Mayor, do ask Mr. Slocum to be our interim sheriff." Samantha's eyes shone with a bright light that almost blinded Slocum. She was in hog heaven now.

"Will you consent to be sworn in two weeks early?" asked the mayor. "It is temporary, of course, pending the outcome of the campaign, but considering the qualities of your opponent, there's not much chance March will get elected."

"Not if we keep him from stuffing the ballot boxes. Remember the last election, mayor, when half of potter's field upped and voted?" Fenneman enjoyed Leroy's uneasiness at mention of falsified voting records. "And not a one of them voters came by my saloon for a drink, either. Damned inconsiderate of them, don't you think?"

Slocum's mind raced as he tried to figure some way out of accepting the badge Jed was handing to George Leroy. He stepped back and held out his hand, shaking his head. He'd rather run his hand into a fire than accept that badge.

"Can't do it, Mayor. Wouldn't look right. Some folks might think I was taking advantage of March in the election. That'd only cause folks to get riled and cause more trouble. A sheriff's got to have everybody backing him. This just isn't right."

"But John, you simply must accept!" protested Samantha. She looked aggrieved that he wouldn't take the badge. "It's only temporary, until the election. Everyone will know that."

"Doesn't matter to me," Slocum said. "I wouldn't feel right, and March will say I'm taking advantage of you good people."

"What about this murderer? You can't let him go free," protested Leroy. "The town is in danger."

"Don't see it that way, Mayor. Whoever killed D—" Slocum caught himself before he put a name to the corpse in the cell. "Whoever killed that cuss is long gone. I couldn't find any sign of him out back. I take that to mean he got on his horse and rode like the wind. Unless I miss my guess, this time next week he'll still be riding away from Van Eyck."

"True," said the mayor, obviously relieved there wasn't likely to be more killing in his town.

Jed whispered just loud enough for Slocum to hear, "And we won't have to pay him if he don't accept the badge."

"Very well, Mr. Slocum. We regret this situation but understand your reasons for not being sworn in right away."

"That means a killer will go unpunished," Samantha said.

"If I can find a trail, I'll start after him at first light," Slocum said. "Think of it as having a sheriff without paying him." He smiled in George Leroy's direction. The mayor flushed and bustled from the jail office. Jed followed close behind.

"Damnedest thing I ever saw, those two. You got to wonder if they're just close friends or maybe asshole buddies." The saloon owner turned and faced Slocum. "And I got to wonder about you. Why not take the job, Slocum? You're gonna be sheriff in a couple weeks." Fenneman scratched his beard.

Before Slocum could answer, a horse's hooves pounded loud and hard outside. The rider dismounted in a flash and filled the entire door. Slocum wasn't sure he had ever seen a bigger man—or one who looked meaner. Shoulders brushing the sides of the door and having to duck when he came through, the man twisted from side to side to keep from catching his two fancy-handled six-guns on the door frame.

Slocum swallowed hard when he saw the Texas Ranger's badge gleaming on the man's vest.

"Where's that no good sheriff of yours?" the ranger boomed in a bass voice. "I got business with Dawkins."

"Ain't here," Fenneman said. "He stole some money and hightailed it. You lookin' for him?"

The ranger snorted in disgust. "I'm after a pair of real outlaws name of Barstow and Dunphy. Heard rumors there might be a third one riding with them, but I can't say more on that."

Slocum went cold inside. Whatever his former partners had done to get a ranger after them caused him a world of trouble. That the ranger hadn't identified him by name meant little. The lawman might have only a vague description.

"Maybe we have one of them in the cell, Ranger," said Samantha. "Back there."

The ranger pushed past Slocum and stared at Dunphy's body. He came back and stated, "That's Dunphy. Did Barstow do it? Wouldn't put it past that sneaky sidewinder to kill his own partner."

"We didn't even know that mangy cayuse's name till you identified him just now," said Fenneman. "You reckon this

Barstow fellow upped and killed him?"

"Doesn't much matter. I'll get him, and maybe the third one, too. How long since that one got shot?" The ranger had the coldest eyes Slocum had ever seen. It didn't much matter to the ranger if he took Barstow in alive or dead, but he'd get him or die trying.

Slocum wondered how many slugs from a Winchester it would take to kill this mountain of muscle and mean.

"Been an hour or more," Slocum lied. He wanted the trail to seem colder than it was.

"That's right, Ranger," said Fenneman. "Slocum here looked and looked but couldn't find any sign of the killer."

Slocum shifted weight slightly to be able to draw if the ranger showed any sign of recognition at his name. The huge man was lost in his own thoughts, maybe mentally riding ahead, figuring how best to track down Barstow.

"You don't have a badge, so you're not the town sheriff," the ranger said.

"He is running for sheriff." Samantha didn't seem the least cowed by the tall ranger's cold glare. As he studied her fine figure and perfect face, the lawman relaxed a mite.

"Sorry to be so brusque, ma'am. Name's Ralston and I ride with the Texas Rangers out of El Paso." He tipped his dusty, broad-brimmed hat in Samantha's direction.

She introduced herself and started in on pleasantries that quickly palled on Ranger Ralston.

"Best to find a place to sleep, Mrs. Clairmont. I've been on the trail for a week or more and I'm plumb tuckered out. Want to go after Barstow when it's light." The gigantic ranger left the office, again brushing his broad shoulders on either side of the door. Slocum was tempted to draw and start putting bullets into Ralston's spine, hoping that a healthy dose of lead might bring the huge lawman down. He didn't want Ralston on his trail.

And that was what was likely to happen if—when—Ralston found Barstow. A coward and double-crossing snake like Barstow would spill his guts if he thought it might get him a moment's consideration. Slocum had

seen the ranger's like before. Men like that knew every
Comanche torture and used them to get information from
their captives.

Barstow would be confessing and writing Slocum's name
in his own blood when Ralston got down to asking the hard
questions.

"What's wrong, John? You look worried," said Samantha.

"Didn't expect to see a Texas Ranger come through Van
Eyck," Slocum said. There wasn't any reason to tangle with
an organization that never quit hunting until they brought
their man to justice—*their* kind of justice. He'd never heard
of a ranger allowing a lynching, but the prisoners they
brought in were often more dead than alive. And they were
persistent. This kept ringing in Slocum's head.

"It must be a comfort to know you won't have to find
this Barstow person all by yourself," Samantha said. "Let
the ranger bring him to justice. With a killing added to his
crimes, he is sure to be removed from society."

Slocum worried that Barstow wasn't the only one to be
removed from civilized company. He considered telling
Jenks the bank robbery was off, then thought harder. Adam
Jenks wasn't the kind of man who much cared about long
shots. He'd see the ranger's presence as a challenge instead
of a danger.

And Slocum wasn't about to fess up to Jenks about riding
with Barstow and Dunphy. The fewer people who could tie
him and Barstow together, the better. Slocum knew from
experience there wasn't any honor among thieves. He didn't
think Jenks would turn him in for the reward, whatever it
might be, but he didn't know about the other three riding
with Jenks. And the outlaw leader would turn in his own
grandmother if it meant saving his hide.

"I've changed my mind," Slocum said suddenly. "Does
the mayor have to swear me in as sheriff or can I just pin
on the badge?"

Fenneman let out a whoop of glee, and Samantha
Clairmont studied him closely, the shadow of a smile
dancing on her lips. Slocum wondered what that meant—
or if he'd live long enough to find out.

10

Slocum shifted impatiently from foot to foot, not wanting there to be any ceremony. Mayor Leroy insisted, seeing a chance for bolstering his own image, and had alerted half the town. Slocum kept looking toward the horizon where the sun peeped up, promising another scorching day. He wanted to be on the trail after Barstow. Ranger Ralston had left a good hour earlier. From the comments the huge man had made, he knew how to track.

"By the power vested in me—" George Leroy stopped when his assistant nudged him in the ribs. Jed whispered frantically for several seconds. Leroy tried to shake off whatever Jed was saying, but his assistant kept talking. Finally, the mayor frowned and turned back to Slocum.

"Let me start over on this ceremony. I hereby swear you in as sheriff of the township of Van Eyck, Texas." The mayor scratched Slocum with the tip of the pin holding the badge on his shirt front. Slocum had always thought wearing a badge had to be uncomfortable. He didn't know it was painful, too.

"Thanks, Mayor, for your confidence in me," Slocum said. "Now I got to be going if I want to find the man who killed my prisoner." The words burned Slocum's tongue. He even sounded like a lawman. In all the years he'd ridden the trail after leaving his farm in Georgia, he had never met but one or two lawmen he liked and respected. The breed and he didn't travel well together.

Now he had joined their rank, even if it was a sham.

"Nonsense, John, make a better speech than that. The people expect it," urged Samantha Clairmont. She had gathered her women's group. They stood by their menfolks, occasionally elbowing them to keep attention focused on the ceremony.

At the back of the small crowd his opponent stood and fumed. Slocum watched the storm clouds of anger darken March's face and wondered what devilment the would-be sheriff would cause. It didn't matter much to him. All he had to do was track down Barstow and get rid of him, then return to Van Eyck in time to be sure the railroad's payroll was safely stashed in the bank.

Then he'd be rich and riding with the wind to get the hell away from Van Eyck. Barstow and Dunphy would have gotten their just desserts and there'd be no reason to look back.

"I'm so proud of you, John," said Samantha, her powerful fingers clutching at his arm. When he looked down, she hastily pulled away, hiding her hands under a large drawstring purse and averting her eyes as if she'd been caught doing something naughty. For a genteel lady, her hands were mighty rough.

The widow woman complicated his life more than Slocum wanted to admit. She had fire and intelligence and beauty and all the other things Slocum wanted in a woman, but he wished he could see past the screen she pulled shut between them. At times he felt closer to her than he had to any other woman in years, only to have her withdraw just enough to leave him guessing.

"We're counting on you to do good things for the town, Slocum," spoke up Fenneman. "And in way of celebrating our new sheriff, drinks are on me!"

This got the men in the crowd moving. The women looked after them with some disdain but said nothing as they hurried off to take up the saloon owner on his generous offer. Slocum didn't follow. The mayor caught his eye and motioned him to one side.

"Uh, Mr. Slocum." George Leroy cleared his throat. "Allow me to amend that. *Sheriff* Slocum, there is a small matter I need to discuss with you in private." Slocum noticed that Jed hadn't withdrawn. The mayor's fawning lapdog was starting to irritate him.

"What is it? I need to get moving if I want to catch Barstow before he gets too far away."

"Don't worry so about him. We might be needing your services closer at hand. It was a nasty business that murder in the jail, but the Texas Ranger can take care of it better than you." The mayor turned pale when he realized he had just insulted Slocum's abilities.

"That's not exactly what Mayor Leroy meant, Sheriff," spoke up Jed. "He means you might consider staying in town to deal with our increasing crimes of violence. Why just last night—"

"I'm going to fetch that murdering son of a bitch," Slocum said, cutting off Jed. "There's not been that much trouble in Van Eyck since I arrived."

"Precisely my point. You prevent it. But that's not exactly what I needed to tell you. There's a matter of our town's impecuniosity."

"What?"

"We don't have money to pay your salary. That's what the mayor's trying to tell you," spoke up Jed. Slocum ignored him.

"I'm not doing this for the money. I told you that last night."

"But you changed your mind. I thought it was the lure of easy money." The mayor was confused.

Slocum had to laugh harshly. He didn't cotton much to being Sheriff Slocum, but he'd never thought of the job as a way to get rich. Most farmers earned better money and did it without the risk of getting shot in the back.

"Keep your money. We'll discuss it after the election."

Mayor Leroy let out a sigh of relief and Jed smirked so much Slocum wanted to push his face in. He turned from the blustering politicians and ran smack into Samantha.

"This isn't part of your job, but I understand your reasons

for finding this Barstow person and bringing him to justice,"
she said. He had the feeling she was teasing him again.

"What do you mean?"

"Why," she said guilelessly, long eyelashes batting over
blue eyes, "it is an affront that your prisoner was killed in
your very own jail. Any self-respecting man has to respond
by bringing the miscreant to the fate he deserves."

Slocum's head was hurting from all the fine words spewed
out by the mayor and Samantha. He tipped his hat in her
direction and said, "I'll be back in a few days. Don't reckon
it'll be longer, one way or the other."

"Be careful, John," she said, and this time he felt her
sincerity. He wanted to kiss her, but that just wasn't done
in public, not to a proper woman.

He nodded and rushed off to get his horse saddled. He'd
have to ride like hell to find Barstow before the ranger.
Otherwise, he might as well keep on riding and never see
Samantha again.

Slocum thought he had an idea what direction Barstow
might take when he left. He and Dunphy had holed up
after the stagecoach robbery. If Barstow had ridden out
the storm of Sheriff Tallant's hunt, he might feel safe
going back. And if he had gone in any other direction,
Slocum had to give up any hope of finding him. It might
be for the best if Barstow hightailed it for Mexico and
was never seen again, but Slocum didn't think it would
happen.

Men like Barstow kept turning up like bad pennies.

Slocum rode steadily, carefully watching for any sign of
the ranger, Barstow, or the sheriff who had been so eager
to stretch his neck after the stagecoach robbery. In the back
of his mind, Slocum knew he ought to be wary of Apaches,
too. They had saved him with their flaming arrows and the
cryptic map that had gotten him out of the box canyon. But
something told him he wasn't likely to find them, and he
couldn't put a decent reason to his guess.

He crossed a trail just after noon and kept riding along it
until his gelding began to tire. Slocum dropped down and

had a meal of beans and peaches while he waited out the hottest part of the day. He tried to rest but the heat and need to get after Barstow kept him from sleeping more than a few minutes at a stretch. Finally deciding the stifling heat had died enough, he mounted up again and struck pay dirt almost immediately.

Fresh horse manure marked where a rider had passed less than an hour earlier. Slocum picked up the pace and crested a rise.

He looked down the barrels of two six-shooters.

"Howdy, Ranger," Slocum greeted. He hadn't realized he was this close to the ranger's path. The lawman had taken some time out to camp and let the day's heat die down a mite before continuing, and Slocum had come up on him.

"You're the fellow from back in Van Eyck. You were running for town sheriff."

Slocum was suddenly glad to have the badge pinned on his shirt. "They swore me in early," he said. "Prisoner killing doesn't set well with anyone in town. I'm out here to find Barstow."

"Reckon I did mention the sidewinder's name," Ralston said. He studied Slocum another few seconds, then spun his pistols back into their holsters in a flashy move. Slocum wasn't impressed. The big man moved well, but Slocum thought he might be able to take him in a face-to-face gunfight. He thought he was just a tad quicker.

He hoped it didn't come to that, though. This ranger was one mean customer.

"I've been following Barstow's trail since noon when I saw your tracks," Slocum said, dismounting. His horse let out a nicker of relief at the load being taken from its back.

"Mighty good tracking, if you followed him that long. How'd you know what direction he'd take?"

"A little luck, a little skill. How'd you know?"

Ralston's expression never changed as he said, "A lot of luck, a lot of skill."

"How far ahead do you reckon he is?" Slocum asked.

"Even if he rode all night, he couldn't be too much ahead of us. Traveling after dark, without much of a moon to light the way, is dangerous. He has to know his horse might step in a prairie dog hole."

Ralston finished the dregs of his cold coffee and threw the bitter remains onto the ground. He watched as it evaporated in the hot sun. He finally said, "He can't be too far ahead. Why don't you go on back to town and let me handle this?"

"My jail, my prisoner that got killed," said Slocum. He remembered what the mayor had said about pride and duty. "I can't get off to a start like that. They'd take my badge back in a flash."

Slocum wasn't sincere enough in his declaration of duty. Ralston sneered a mite, then packed his few belongings and heaved the saddlebags over his horse's hindquarters. He was ready to ride in a few minutes.

"Come along if you like. I won't wait up for you."

Slocum didn't know whether to laugh or take offense. He was one of the best damned trackers in Texas. He wouldn't hold the ranger back. Then he realized the ranger thought he was nothing more than a small hick town sheriff.

"I'll try to keep up," Slocum said, figuring his chances of shooting both the ranger and Barstow. It might not come to that if the ranger got to the fleeing outlaw first. From the look of the two six-shooters the ranger carried, he knew how to fight. If Barstow put up any resistance, he was likely to be buzzard bait in the time it took for two bullets to rip through his heart.

Slocum picked up Barstow's trail before the ranger did. He started to point it out when he saw a cloud of dust rising ahead. Barstow had left the trail and curved south and west. The fuss ahead had to be caused by at least five riders, maybe more. There hadn't been any sign of the Apaches. That meant Slocum might be riding into the waiting arms of Sheriff Tallant's posse.

"There's the trail," Slocum said, pointing to the southeast. "He left the trail here and took off for that pile of rock. He might think to stand us off there."

Slocum cursed his bad luck. If he had spoken a few seconds earlier, he might have convinced the ranger to follow the bogus trail. Not now. Ralston had picked up Barstow's trail with the skill of a well-trained bloodhound.

"Wrong way," the ranger said. "He rode this direction."

Slocum tried not to look at the dust cloud moving ever closer. There were at least five riders, maybe more. He couldn't remember how many had been in Tallant's posse, but that cloud might be theirs. Ralston hadn't seen it, working on Barstow's spoor.

"This way. I'm sure."

"You've got good instincts," Ralston said, as close to a compliment as anything Slocum was likely to get from the man, "but you're wrong. The trail goes that way." Ralston pointed out the bright scratch on a rock left by a horseshoe.

"If you don't mind, I'll just go this way."

"May the best man find the scoundrel," Ralston said, turning his horse in the direction Barstow had taken. Slocum positioned himself so that the ranger had to look away from the dust cloud. Slocum saw how it settled, as if the riders weren't making as good a time now, or possibly had ridden across a rocky stretch of desert.

Ralston rode on without another word, eyes fixed on the spoor he had found. Slocum wasted no time urging his tired horse in the other direction. He didn't want to find out if his hunch about the distant riders was right.

Slocum rode fast and hard for almost five minutes, then slowly reined back and let his gelding catch its breath. He turned away from the pile of rocks he had pointed out as Barstow's possible hideout and circled to approach the riders he thought to be Sheriff Tallant's posse from the east. He had to keep close enough to Ralston so Barstow wouldn't fall into the ranger's capable hands, but he had to be even more cautious than he wanted.

Riding into the setting sun made the going harder for Slocum. He pulled the brim of his hat down to shade his eyes and then had to look up often to be sure he wasn't riding into the jaws of a trap. The terrain cooperated with him, affording him many arroyos and rocky ravines to ride down, keeping him hidden from anyone ahead. In an hour he found the trail of the riders he had spotted.

He dropped to hands and knees and studied the trail left in the shifting sand. Wind had removed some traces, but he saw that five men had ridden shod horses past this spot. No Apaches. Posse? Probably. Slocum cursed the sheriff's tenacity. He must be angling to get into the Texas Rangers.

Slocum looked up when he heard voices. He studied the ground again and knew he wasn't wrong. The riders had been here a full hour ahead. Whose voices?

He tethered his horse and crept forward, dropping flat on his belly when he heard an angry argument. He pulled off his hat and poked his head over the top of a rocky rise. Not a hundred feet away Ralston stood with his arms crossed over his barrel chest, the vision of a mountain refusing to be moved.

"You don't have any call going after my man, Ranger," declared a shorter, thinner man. He stood so close he looked up into Ralston's face, not the least bit awed by either the ranger's size or his badge. "I got the warrant for Barstow. He's mine, I say."

"He's wanted down Austin way. If I find him, he's mine. You can have him after he's stood trial for killing a lawyer."

"So when's that a crime? He robbed a bank in Fort Davis, and I want him for that. Then him and Dunphy and another galoot held up a stage. I want them bad for that."

"Dunphy's dead. What about the other gent you're looking for? The one who rode with Barstow?"

Sheriff Tallant laughed harshly. "He was turned in by some drunk in Fort Davis. The drunk staggered up and told us about the stagecoach robbery. Didn't get a name or description, but there was three of 'em what held up the stage. And they're mine, Ranger. Mine!"

"Dunphy's all yours. He's pushing up posies over in Van Eyck. Don't know about the third one, but Barstow's around here somewhere. I'd stake my reputation on it."

"You find him, he's mine," Tallant insisted.

"He'll be yours after he stands trial for killing the law-yer." Ralston smiled crookedly and added, "It was his own lawyer he upped and killed."

"Don't care if he killed everyone in the state of Texas."

Their voices lowered, and Slocum realized that both Ralston and Tallant had lost Barstow's trail. He edged away, grateful for this unexpected piece of luck. He still had a chance of finding Barstow before either the sheriff or the ranger.

But it was getting dark and he couldn't risk blundering into either of the lawmen. Slocum mounted his horse and rode south a ways, then turned and went west. He had a few ideas where Barstow might have holed up, and come morning he'd see how good at outthinking the backshooting son of a bitch he was.

11

Slocum stirred fitfully, a fly buzzing around his face. He swatted it away. Then he came completely awake when he heard the distinctive click of a shell being chambered in a rifle. He grabbed for his Colt, but a boot crushed his wrist to the ground.

"Try that again and we'll ventilate you, mister," came the cold warning.

Slocum still wasn't completely awake. He sank back, working his hand out from under the boot. He stared up into four rifle barrels, each looking bigger than the last.

The Lipan Apaches and their flaming arrows weren't going to rescue him this time. Whatever happened would be the result of his fast action or silver tongue.

"What's going on, Sheriff?" he asked, directing his question at the man standing apart from the others. Slocum had never seen Sheriff Tallant up close, and he wasn't sure he liked what he saw very much. The sheriff had a narrow, mean face and a mustache badly in need of tending. The loose ends had turned into a wire brush and went every which way. A front tooth was missing and another had been covered over with gold, giving Tallant an even stranger aspect. The prominent bandage on his arm showed where Slocum had winged him in the fight back in the box canyon. Slocum's only regret was that he hadn't taken the lawman's damned head off with the shot.

"I reckon you're going to tell us you're just an innocent traveler, that you just happened to be camping here in the desert. Is that what you're going to say?" Tallant thrust out his chest as if puffing up would intimidate Slocum more than the four rifles still aimed at his head.

"Couldn't be farther from the truth," Slocum said. He moved slowly and showed the badge pinned onto his shirt. "I'm out looking for a bushwhacker that killed a prisoner in my jail." Slocum almost spat out the words. It wasn't "his" jail and Dunphy hadn't been "his" prisoner in the strictest sense. He would have tortured Dunphy to get him to talk. Slocum had known a lawman or two who'd do the same to get a confession, but Slocum would never have used Dunphy's words against him in a court of law.

Barstow had beat him to the trigger.

"You don't have the look of a lawman, does he, men?" Tallant's squinty eyes never left Slocum.

"Can't say he does, Sheriff. I seen my share of men wearing badges, and he don't look comfortable with it on. What are we going to do with him?" The man's finger played with the rifle's trigger until Slocum got a bit worried. He might not live long enough to have his neck stretched by a hangman's rope.

Slocum moved like a striking rattler. His leg kicked out and caught one deputy behind the knee. The man tried to keep his balance by throwing up his hands. Somewhere along the way his rifle discharged. Slocum rolled, inches away from a pair of slugs that ripped through his bedroll. He kept rolling until he fetched up against a rock, then he jerked in the other direction. A third shot missed him, sending splinters of rock in a dusty cascade over him.

He bowled over a second deputy and was rewarded with a rifle butt on the side of the head. Sheriff Tallant swung a second time and dropped Slocum to the ground.

"Now that's as close to a confession as we're likely to see, men," the sheriff said. "We can take him back to Fort Davis for trial or we can just string him up over the limb of the nearest cottonwood."

"Seen one a mile back," the deputy said from the ground. Anger reddened his face. He wanted revenge on Slocum for making him look like a fool. "It's been a spell, but I still remember how to tie a hangman's knot."

"Don't need much fancy rope tying," Tallant said. "Maybe just a loop around his neck. They kick and scream a mite longer. Strangle to death in a few minutes, I reckon, but it saves time tying all those fancy ass turns."

Slocum knew the sheriff was trying to spook him. He gauged distances and chances and prepared to make another escape attempt. Just as he tensed, the sheriff swung his rifle again, this time laying the barrel alongside Slocum's head. Stars exploded in unknown constellations, and Slocum sagged back to the ground.

"You surely are spirited, I'll give you that. Put the manacles on him." Tallant stood back a few paces and watched. Any hope Slocum might have had at escape was gone now. The heavy chains weighed him down. Even if he got away from the posse, he'd never make it through the desert wearing this much iron. "You want to walk to your hanging or you gonna ride like a man?"

"I'll ride," Slocum said, still trying to figure how to get away. It didn't look as if Tallant had identified him. The sheriff had chanced on him sleeping and decided he must be someone worth stringing up. There might still be a chance to talk his way out of this predicament.

"Don't go tellin' me my business, mister," Tallant said, cutting him off. "You're gonna spin some wild ass lie about being innocent. One look at you and any jury'd know you're guilty as sin."

"Of what crime?" Slocum asked. The deputy helped him onto his horse, but he didn't hand Slocum the reins. He was being led along like a young boy on his first horse.

"You might be the third party to a stagecoach robbery a few days back. We chased that galoot into a canyon, but he gave us the slip. Still don't know how he done that." Tallant squinted even more, looking downright feral. He rubbed his wound and the tips of his mustaches twitched in anger at his memories. "You want to tell us how you got out of the canyon?"

"Can't help you on that, Sheriff, because I'm not your man. I was just sworn in as sheriff over in Van Eyck. You can ride over that way and find out."

"Anything to keep from kicking your heels in midair, is that it?" Tallant shook his head, making his mustaches whip about in the wind like they'd come alive. "Well, mister, it ain't gonna work. If we rode back to Fort Davis without something to report, we'd be the laughingstock of the town."

"Already pretty bad," said a deputy. "Half the posse went back after they got shot up."

"One man shot up half your posse?" asked Slocum. "Must be one mean hombre."

"Apaches, it was them Apaches," the deputy declared sullenly. "We didn't know we was runnin' into a den of them."

"Haven't seen hide nor hair of any Apaches in months," Slocum lied. "You sure it just wasn't that man you were chasing who did you in like that?" He wanted to needle them into making a mistake, just as Tallant had tried to trick him into admitting something only the stagecoach robber would have known.

It didn't work any better for Slocum than it had for the sheriff.

"There's a good-sized tree, Sheriff," a deputy called out. "You really want us to string 'im up?"

Slocum waited for the sheriff's answer. This might be a bluff on the lawman's part. Then he saw the cold eyes and knew it wasn't. Tallant didn't much care who he killed if he could return to his home town with stories of bravery and road agents dispatched.

"We string 'im up. Sorry, mister. You put up a right good fight, but it wasn't much better an attempt than that stage robbery you, Barstow, and Dunphy tried."

"I'm on Barstow's trail," Slocum said, holding down a tide of rising panic. "He's the one who killed Dunphy in my jail. In Van Eyck."

"You got a right fine imagination," Tallant said. He sat impassively, watching a deputy knot a rope and swing it over a high limb. The deputy dropped to the ground and fastened it around the cottonwood's thick trunk. Slocum couldn't take his eyes off the loop of rope slowly twisting in the hot wind blowing off the desert. In a few short minutes he'd be weighing down that rope and swinging, too.

"You got any last words, mister?" Tallant sounded perfunctory. He had asked that a dozen times and didn't give two hoots about the answer.

"You always hang other lawmen?" asked Slocum.

"You can playact all you want. We got you dead to rights." Tallant laughed harshly. "Fact of the matter is, we got you dead. Get him moving," ordered the Fort Davis sheriff.

Slocum winced as the rough rope slid over his head. The deputy almost took off his ears as he positioned the noose, but Slocum didn't figure he'd need those ears in a few more minutes. His gelding stirred restlessly. The horse had spotted a succulent clump of buffalo grass and wanted to graze. Slocum hoped the horse would hold still a little longer.

"The fact of the matter is," came a cold voice tinged with just enough mockery to bring Tallant swinging around in the saddle, "you don't know your ass from a hole in the ground."

"This is none of your concern, Ranger," the sheriff said. "We found one of our stagecoach robbers, and we're takin' care of him all properlike."

"Manacles like you got on him would go for five, ten dollars down in Austin. You thinkin' of leaving them on him after he's hung?"

"What are you saying?" demanded Tallant.

"You're fixing to hang the sheriff from over in Van Eyck. What kind of example you be setting for others? If they take it into their heads hanging sheriffs is all proper, how long before somebody's playin' cat's cradle with your neck?"

"He wasn't lyin'? He's really a sheriff?" The deputy snorted in contempt. "Never seen his like bein' any kind of sheriff."

"He's on the trail of Barstow for killing a prisoner—Dunphy." Ralston rode around and peered straight at Slocum. The huge ranger filled Slocum's entire field of vision. Struggling to keep his chin up and the rough hemp rope from cutting into his flesh, Slocum found himself at the edge of death.

"Decided you were on the wrong trail, Ranger?" Slocum asked. "Told you I was right."

Ralston laughed heartily. Slocum had wondered what the giant of a man found funny. Would he laugh any harder if Slocum's neck was stretched a few more inches by the noose?

"Get that noose off him," Ralston said in his booming voice. "I do declare, you folks haven't got a lick of sense."

"Do it," Tallant said in a sulky voice. He didn't like being told he was wrong, and he especially didn't like missing the opportunity to string up somebody.

Slocum tried not to fall out of the saddle when they pulled the rope from around his neck. With his hands manacled behind him, he was still in a precarious spot, but now he could breathe, and letting his horse graze a mite posed no deadly problems.

"Why don't you just let him keep those manacles as a souvenir?" suggested Ralston. "He ought to have something to show for this morning's shoddy work."

"Get them off his wrists," snarled Tallant. "You come ridin' in here, Ralston, and think you own the country. You don't. I don't care if you are a ranger. We handle lawbreakers in our own way."

"Reckon that's true," Ralston said, "seeing as how you spend all your time stringing up fellow lawmen and letting the criminals go scot-free, you surely do handle the law different out here."

Slocum wondered if the ranger had crossed the line where Tallant had to act or be too humiliated. With the three deputies at his side, the sheriff had the upper hand.

But the staring match lasted only a few seconds. Tallant backed off and motioned for a deputy to return Slocum's ebony-handled Navy Colt.

"What you boys going to do the rest of the day?" Ralston asked. "Heard tell there's a deputy down south lookin' to be strung up. You might find him down Alpine way." Ralston laughed again.

"Barstow's ours," Tallant said. "And this one's not much of a sheriff. He'll make a mistake and then no judge this side of hell will let him off."

"Don't have any quarrel with that," the ranger said. "Just let there be a judge next time." His words carried the blast of a blue norther whipping across the plains.

Tallant and his deputies rode off without another word. Slocum rubbed the burn marks on his throat but didn't go so far as to thank Ralston. This wasn't the kind of man who expected gratitude.

"You lose Barstow's trail?" Slocum asked, checking his pistol and settling his bandanna to cover the rope marks.

"He's slippery, that one, but he'll make a mistake. I got to get back to a town to report. I only had till sunup today to find him."

"You be going back to El Paso then?" Slocum asked, trying not to sound too hopeful.

"We never let a killer get away. I need more information about him, that's all."

They rode in silence. Slocum couldn't keep his attention from the box canyon where he had almost been trapped as they rode past. Cutting through the crevice at the rear of the canyon might cut a day's ride off their return to Van Eyck, but he wasn't about to tell the ranger about the escape cranny. He might need it again someday soon.

"You see any trace of Apaches?"

Ralston turned and stared at him with his marblelike black eyes. "You mean recently?"

"Within the last week or two. Lipan Apaches. Any feathers off their arrows, arrows, any spoor at all?"

"That's a strange thing to ask," Ralston said. "Haven't seen an Apache in months. Most are on their reservations and don't stray too far, leastwise not down into Texas. There's been a few who snuck away from Bosque Redondo up in New Mexico Territory, but they know better than to come this far south."

"Might be heading for Mexico."

"There're quicker routes across the Rio Grande," Ralston said. He sank into a silence so complete nothing could entice him out of it. This suited Slocum just fine. It took them two days getting back to Van Eyck, and he knew from the banners he saw strung across the streets he probably wasn't the front-runner in the election anymore.

12

"Looks like you're not doing too good in getting elected," Ralston said, eyeing the dozens of colorful banners proclaiming March to be the only native candidate for sheriff worth a bucket of warm spit. Other banners carried more vicious reminders that drifters caused Van Eyck's troubles and hinted that Slocum would only increase the number coming to town.

"They don't realize their town's well nigh dead and barely kicking," Slocum said. "When the railroad is done with Van Eyck, this street will be nothing but weeds and memories."

"Got to wire El Paso and see what I'm to do next," Ralston said. He rode off without another word. The two-day trip into town had been spent mostly in silence. Ralston hadn't inquired about Slocum's past, and for that small bit of luck Slocum was vastly relieved. He didn't want to lie constantly. That always tripped a man up if the listener paid any attention, and the ranger was intent. Ralston preferred to keep his own company, though.

Slocum reined back and dismounted in front of Fenneman's saloon, making sure his gelding was near the watering trough. Slocum had been in the saddle almost a week and was sore, tired, and badly in need of a shot or two of whiskey. Even Fenneman's vile, gut-burning trade whiskey would go quite a way toward cutting the dust that had caked in the back of his throat.

"There you are, Slocum. We missed you. You get that bushwhacker?" Fenneman sat at the end of the long bar in his usual tailor-style pose. How an old man like him managed to bend his legs into such a knot was beyond Slocum.

"Ran into too much trouble to keep on his trail." Slocum didn't want to tell how close he had come to getting his neck stretched by Sheriff Tallant and his posse. "Give me a shot of whiskey, the good stuff if there's any left."

"That bad a time, eh?" Fenneman slid off the bar and dropped behind, rummaging among the bottles. He fished out four and began pouring from each in turn until he had a couple fingers' worth in the smallest bottle. "The railroad's going to be a boon, yes, sir, it is. We can get good whiskey straight from Kaintuck and Tennessee."

"The railroad's going to kill this town and you know it," Slocum said, in no mood to spin tall yarns about the future of Van Eyck. He watched as Fenneman poured a glass full and looked longingly at it before sliding it over.

It went down smoother than silk. "Thanks," Slocum said. "I do appreciate it. I know you don't have much of this left."

"This is about all I have. Don't much matter how many cases I order. They just never arrive. Shipping damage, they say. Thirsty sons of bitches along the way, I say."

Slocum savored the warmth and let his thoughts drift: Adam Jenks; Samantha Clairmont; the bank.

"You're getting a faraway look in your eye. The job too much for you?"

"Doesn't look as if I'll be sheriff much longer, not with the election next week."

"Don't put too much store in March's banners. He talks a good game, but when it comes down to bein' sheriff, he'll be a colossal failure."

It didn't matter to Slocum. He wasn't cut out to be a sheriff and he knew it. Letting March elect himself was a godsend. "What about the people? They eager for a new sheriff?"

"They'll go to anybody's rally if enough free beer is

served. What goes on during the voting's what matters. If you'd brought back Dunphy's killer, now, that would have cinched the election for you." Fenneman canted his head to one side. "What went on out there?"

"Nothing but a small territorial dispute. The sheriff from Fort Davis is hot under the collar to find Barstow, too." Slocum wondered if he ought to ask for the last shot in the bottle. Fenneman had worked to hoard this much. To drink a second shot of such a precious, smooth liquid seemed almost a sacrilege.

"I'll save this for the celebration when you win," Fenneman said, putting a cork in the bottle and shoving it back under the bar. "Got plenty of the rotgut whiskey."

Slocum tapped the side of his glass to indicate he needed it. Fenneman poured without comment. Slocum put away two more before the memory of the rope around his neck faded. He knew he ought not to get worked up over the sheriff's insistence on hanging him, but he couldn't help it. Tallant's name was added to the list, just under Barstow's. But first the railroad payroll, then the revenge. He had been lured away from his real purpose in Van Eyck.

"Not a whole lot going on in town since you took after Barstow," said Fenneman. "Whole town's buzzing about the payroll coming in a couple days from now. Ought to be a big blowout to celebrate. The railroad workers will be following their money in and should spend most of it right here."

"You got enough barrels of this filthy liquor to get them drunk?" Slocum indicated the bottle on the bar. He was a bit tipsy. He hadn't eaten much while on the trail, and the whiskey was eating away like acid at his belly.

"More'n enough, Slocum, more'n enough," Fenneman assured him. Louder, the barkeep said, "You wantin' a drink, too, Ranger?"

"Just one. I got to hit the trail again." Ralston sidled up to the bar next to Slocum. "I wired El Paso and got new orders. Got to stop some Mexican bandidos from crossing the Rio Grande and rustling cattle on a spread a ways south of the Big Bend."

"You're giving up on Barstow?" Slocum hardly dared to hope for such luck.

"For the time being I'll be on this new assignment. But I never give up. If they try to send me on some other cockamamie mission, I'll take time off and bring Barstow in on my own. He's like a nettle under my saddle blanket. The longer I ride, the worse he digs in and irritates me. Nobody gets away from me. Nobody." Ralston stared at Slocum with eyes like flat black glass. Whatever thoughts went on in the ranger's head Slocum couldn't say. He wouldn't want to play poker with this man.

Ralston knocked back the drink and left the saloon without so much as a fare thee well. Slocum heaved a sigh of relief at the sight of the big ranger's back going out the door. Around Ralston he felt as if he was foolishly throwing blasting caps against a wall and waiting for one to explode in his face.

"Not a man to cross," Fenneman observed. "You want another, Slocum?"

"This will do me for the time. Thanks." Slocum fished out the wad of greenbacks he had taken from Dunphy and paid for the whiskey. It seemed appropriate that some of the money from the stage robbery ended up doing him some good.

He stretched when he got outside on the boardwalk. Hot wind blew down the street, causing March's banners to flutter and snap. He hadn't spared any expense stringing the red-white-and-blue standards where every voting citizen could see them. Slocum walked slowly, trying to ignore them. March wasn't going to buy the election, though he stood a better chance of winning since Slocum had failed to bring back Dunphy's killer.

Slocum was almost bowled over as Samantha hurried from the general store. The collision caused her to drop a wrapped package.

"Why, John, I didn't know you'd returned," she said, bending to pick up her newly purchased goods.

"Let me," Slocum said. He got to the small bundle before the woman could desperately grab it. The paper had torn.

He saw a pair of heavy work gloves.

"Thank you," she said, snatching it away from him. "I have to get back to Mrs. Parman's now, but let's get together later." She stood and her blue eyes twinkled. "It hasn't been *too* long, John." Samantha moved a bit closer. Anyone standing even a few feet away couldn't have seen how she reached out and stroked the bulge at his crotch. She smiled wickedly and said, "But it seems to be getting long now, don't you agree?"

"Dinner," he suggested. "You can tell me what's been going on in town. Looks as if March is carrying the voters in his direction with all his signs."

"Oh, pooh," she said. "Don't you believe it. He is buying their attention right now. You have something better to offer than free liquor and food and fancy pennants. Call for me at seven?" She batted her eyes, and Slocum nodded agreement.

Samantha pulled her parcels in close to her body and hurried off. She stopped at the end of the boardwalk and looked back over her shoulder. The hot desert wind blew a stand of her blond hair back, making Slocum think of the campaign banners March had put up. Anyone seeing this banner, though, would never notice anything else around him. She gave Slocum a quick parting smile and turned down an alley on her way to the boardinghouse.

Slocum started to keep walking, but his steps slowed and he found himself returning to the store. He went inside, grateful for the dim coolness.

"Howdy, Sheriff. What can I get for you?" The storekeeper waited patiently behind the counter, as if he was riveted to the spot.

"I've got a bit of a problem," Slocum said. "Mrs. Clairmont was supposed to buy something for me, and I think she got it wrong. I wanted to check to be sure, just in case she's been here."

"You missed her by a couple minutes," the shopkeeper said. "I'd've thought you two would have seen each other outside."

"Didn't," Slocum lied.

"Well then, she did buy another pair of work gloves."

"That's what she was getting me. I'd asked her to see to them before I left town."

"That's the bin where she got 'em." The man pointed to a small tower of boxes, each with a different sized pair of gloves in it. Slocum went over and searched until he found a pair that fit snugly.

"This the size she got?"

"No, no, she got much smaller ones, same as always. That first bin, just under the one where you got those."

Slocum tried on those gloves and couldn't begin to cram his hands into them. He tossed the others back and put his hand over the gloves that matched those Samantha had gotten. They were enough smaller that her strong hands would fit, but why did she need work gloves?

"You said 'same as always.' She's bought gloves before?"

The storekeeper shrugged. "Reckon I've sold her two other pair, same size. I'm sure they're for her. Now that you mention it, why's a cultured lady like her wanting gloves?"

"Her vegetable garden," Slocum said quickly. "Behind the boardinghouse. Surely, she bought some tools to work in the garden?"

"A pick and a shovel when she first came to town," the man said. "I don't remember why she said she was buying them, but she had a good reason. I remember that much."

"When she came to town? I thought Mrs. Clairmont had lived here most of her life."

"Heavens no. She came to town less than two months back. Her husband had just died and left her a tidy sum." The storekeeper frowned as he tried to remember other details. "Can't say much more about her, other than she's one fine lady. Wish there were a dozen more like her in town."

"Thanks," Slocum said.

"Are you going to get those gloves? Or you want me to talk to Mrs. Clairmont about exchanging the ones she got?"

"Don't mention it to her," Slocum said. "I'm sure she's got something in mind."

Slocum walked quickly to Mrs. Parman's and stared at the upstairs window. He and Samantha had made love in that room, but now there didn't seem to be anyone inside. Slocum walked around the boardinghouse, looking for a garden. All he found was a patch of knee-high weeds.

Then he noticed a broad expanse of fresh dirt. He dropped to one knee and picked up a handful. The dirt had been turned over several times, the sun-dried lumps broken, as if someone had prepared the land for a garden. Slocum stood and tried to figure how much land was being readied for cultivation. He paced off in one direction, then turned at right angles and paced off more.

"That's more than a hundred square yards of garden," he said. "A man could do pretty well on that much."

He turned from the garden to the bank next door. The broad brick side called to him. Just a stick or two of dynamite would get through it and reveal the juicy payroll in the steel vault.

Slocum circled the bank, studying it for weak spots. It didn't have any that he could see, other than a banker likely to trust a lawman with a key. Slocum worked on a story to give Mulholland the night of the robbery. Figures seen lurking around the bank. Maybe someone rummaging around inside a teller's cage.

That was more like it, Slocum decided. Someone inside, carrying a small light, as if they were getting ready to open the vault. With a key he, Jenks, and the others could breeze inside and drill the holes needed to blow the vault. Before Mulholland knew what was happening, there would be an unauthorized nighttime withdrawal at the Bank of Van Eyck.

Slocum wasn't sure how far he ought to carry the charade of being a lawman. Maybe he could tell Mulholland he was too late, that he was going after the thieves, and then never return. The townsfolk might think he had been ambushed and killed by the robbers as he chased them. If that was good or bad, Slocum couldn't say. They might mount a posse to bring their sheriff's killers to justice, and then again they might not. March would push himself forward and demand to be deputized. Getting away from the portly March would be as easy as licking butter off a knife.

Only a few days to wait for the payroll. Slocum knew he had to tell Jenks, but he didn't want to go find the outlaw's camp. Not yet, not after being on the trail for a week.

"Well, I do declare. This is a surprise, John. We seem to be bumping into each other all the time." Samantha had left the bank and stood just inside the front door, writing furiously in a small notebook.

"Not enough, if you ask me," he said. "Dinner's a long ways off." He wanted to see what her reaction would be. She bit her lower lip as if considering, then smiled.

"Mrs. Parman is gone right now. I had planned to do some work, but a little pleasure in the afternoon might make the work go faster."

"What work's this?" Slocum asked.

"Don't get too nosy. It's a surprise, and you'll be the first to know of it. Now come along, but don't follow too close. Everyone loves to gossip, and it would destroy your chance of being elected sheriff if March managed to tarnish your reputation."

"Hurting yours would be worse," Slocum said. He couldn't help noticing how her bodice had opened just a tad, revealing the smooth white expanse of her breasts. Samantha moved from side to side in such a way that a second button came undone in a most unchaste fashion. If she kept wiggling like she was, she'd be naked to the waist before they got to the boardinghouse.

"Do you like what you see?" she teased.

"You know I do." Slocum grunted when she turned suddenly and brushed against him. Her fingers found his crotch and squeezed down hard. He gasped at the power of his body's response. He snapped fully erect, and it was painful in his tight britches.

"Let's do something about that," she whispered hotly. Samantha swung around and walked off toward the boardinghouse. Slocum followed, wondering if his reputation really mattered. So what if he lost the election to March? Getting into the bank wouldn't change. March wouldn't take over as sheriff until after the robbery, if the payroll money showed up in the next few days.

And Samantha Clairmont's reputation? The shopkeeper had said she'd been in town less than two months. She could always move on if the people got too upset at her lack of morals.

Samantha entered the boardinghouse and spun, throwing her arms around Slocum's neck. It took him by surprise. He barely managed to kick the door shut with his foot. She kissed him passionately. He hadn't thought it was possible, but he got even harder.

"Samantha, wait. Let's go upstairs and—"

"No, John, here. Now!" She dropped to her knees in front of him and worked feverishly to open his fly buttons. His length popped out and into her mouth. Slocum staggered a little when he felt her hot red lips close around the tip of his manhood. Her tongue surged and swirled, moved and licked, until he was on the brink of exploding. It wasn't possible for him to be more on fire in his loins; no prairie fire burned hotter than the one Samantha caused inside him.

"No more," he moaned. "Can't take more of that, but it feels so damned good." He laced his fingers through her blond hair and began guiding her back and forth in a motion that turned him weak in the knees. He leaned back against the front door for support.

"What if Mrs. Parman comes back?" he gasped out.

Blue eyes turned up and looked at him, merriment dancing in them. Samantha never took her mouth from his organ. She licked and sucked and began doing things that caused Slocum to gasp for mercy. He tried to speak, but words refused to form now. Sagging slightly, he edged down the door. Samantha followed him until he was sitting on the floor.

She hiked up her skirts and again he saw she wasn't wearing anything underneath. He thought it must be cooler for her going around indecently dressed like that. Then she lifted one leg and straddled his waist. Samantha sank down, her softly puckered nether lips now swallowing him whole.

It wasn't cool there. It was hot. Damned hot. And the blond made it even hotter for Slocum when she began swaying back and forth, humming a song so softly he barely heard it. Samantha picked up the song's tempo, her hips working harder, faster, more insistently.

"Do you like this?" she asked, breaking off the song. He saw a flush had risen to her shoulders. With shaking fingers, he reached out and unbuttoned her bodice. The flush extended down to her breasts. Slocum fumbled a moment and found the coppery, hard buttons so lustfully engorged. He squeezed on those fleshy pebbles and gave Samantha a sample of what she was giving him.

She kept him pinned to the floor, but Slocum didn't mind. She was lifting and falling with just the right rhythm now to excite him even more. He cupped her breasts and squeezed, using them as fleshy handles to erotically tell her what he wanted most.

He got it. Hips twisting back and forth as she rose, Samantha crashed back down as hard as she could. Over and over she moved in this delightful way until Slocum wasn't able to restrain himself any longer. He felt his balls tightening and his hidden length stiffening to the bursting point.

Samantha shuddered as desire raced through her. She leaned forward for a moment to savor the sensation, then began wriggling around like she had been before. Slocum could no longer control himself. He crushed her breasts in his hands as he erupted into her clinging interior. For what seemed ages he pumped and then it was over. He turned flaccid quickly, the intensity of the lovemaking past.

"Never been with a woman who did that to me," he said.

Samantha leaned back against his raised knees, using them as a support. She put her hands over his and gently removed them from her breasts. Heaving a deep breath, she looked him square in the eye and said, "It's good between us, John, so damned good."

"You make it sound like it's over."

"No, no, nothing of the sort," she said, "but I do have to return to work. Now you get on out of here, and don't forget dinner tonight at seven."

Her hands slid along his arms. He noticed how hard they seemed for a woman who had nothing more to do all day than sit in her room and watch the people outside in the street. Then he forgot all about it as she kissed him as passionately as she ever had.

She got to her feet and looked down at him. "Tonight, John, we'll do it again tonight. All night long."

Slocum vowed to get the biggest, thickest steak he could find in Van Eyck for dinner. He'd need the energy if they came close to matching the intensity of this lovemaking.

13

Slocum walked on rubbery legs from Mrs. Parman's house. The combination of the whiskey and Samantha Clairmont had been more than his tired body could take. He needed sleep, he needed food, and he wanted more of what the blond offered so willingly. Slocum didn't get too far away from the boardinghouse, though. He paused, turned, and looked back, trying to catch a glimpse of Samantha in her upstairs bedroom.

He wasn't disappointed. He'd have to tell her to shut her curtains. She stripped off her dress and dropped it on the bed, standing buck naked in the center of her room, stretching and posing in front of a mirror. Slocum appreciated the sight, occasionally looking around to see if anyone saw him watching the woman. Everyone had taken cover during the hottest part of the day.

Samantha took a shirt from her wardrobe and donned it. Then she climbed into men's canvas pants. Slocum frowned, wondering what was going on. She rummaged around in her wardrobe some more and then vanished from sight. He stood across the street from the bank, eyes never leaving the boardinghouse. After ten minutes the woman still hadn't left. Another five passed and Slocum decided whatever Samantha was doing, it was inside the house and she wasn't coming out.

He sauntered down the street, tipping his hat to the women and exchanging pleasantries with the men who'd look his way. Not many did. He wondered what March had been telling them about him while he was away. The only thing that worried Slocum was that March was telling them the truth. Whatever lies the politician cooked up wouldn't be as damning as a legitimate wanted poster with Slocum's face on it.

Turning, he stared at the bank. Dynamite. No matter how he connived and planned and changed his mind, it came down to dynamite. They'd need a good amount to get into that bank. Slocum was glad Jenks had the forethought to pack some. He still had to ride out to Jenks's camp and tell the outlaw everything that had happened.

Slocum went to the sheriff's office where there was a small cot beside the desk. He didn't have anywhere else to stay, and there wasn't much reason to waste money on the fleabag hotel down the street. Let the visiting railroad workers stay there—or sleep on the streets. He laid down and was asleep within minutes.

He awoke with a start in early evening. He fumbled out his brother Robert's watch and flipped open the case. It was a few minutes until seven. He'd meant to get a shave at the barber shop and maybe a bath. He was still dirty from the time he'd spent in the desert tracking down Barstow. It wouldn't do to take Samantha to dinner smelling like a pig sty.

The dilemma corrected itself when he hurried to Mrs. Parman's Boardinghouse to get Samantha. He intended to postpone the dinner for a half hour, which ought to give him enough time to bathe. He knocked on the door. The older woman answered.

"Ah, Sheriff Slocum," she said. "I have a note for you."

"Thank you, ma'am, but I'm here for Mrs. Clairmont."

"Why, this note is from her. I am sure she sends her regrets at being called away so suddenly." Mrs. Parman handed Slocum a folded note. He inhaled deeply and Samantha's enticing scent rose from it. He didn't know what perfume she used, but it was distinctive. He remembered how Jenks had commented on it. Distinctive and lingering, a cat marking its territory, he thought.

He quickly scanned the few lines of apology for not being able to have dinner with him. Samantha hadn't said why she was gone, but that she was gone filled Slocum with mixed emotions. He wanted to see her again, but this also gave him the chance to ride to Jenks's camp and palaver with him a spell.

"She doesn't say when she'll return," Slocum said. "Do you know how long Mrs. Clairmont will be gone?"

"Why, heavens, no. She never said. She just upped and raced out about five this afternoon. She's been acting strangely, though. Perhaps it is a family matter."

Slocum took his leave, going straight to the saloon where his gelding was still tethered. He cursed himself for not caring for the animal sooner. His exhaustion from the ride and preoccupation with the robbery—and Samantha—weren't good enough excuses for the horse. One brown eye watched as he approached. The horse neighed loudly and tossed its head accusingly.

"Old fella," Slocum said, "we'll get you curried and fed and then we're off for a little ride." The horse seemed to understand and reacted poorly. It wasn't up for more traveling, not tonight. But Slocum had business and the horse had no choice.

Just before sundown Slocum found the trail leading off the main road. A small cairn of stones marked the road to Adam Jenks's camp, but Slocum spotted the guard long before he got there. He'd have to alert Jenks to the sloppy way the man silhouetted himself against the setting sun. With Tallant still prowling around and Ralston threatening to return to find Barstow, anything the least suspicious would draw the lawmen like shit draws flies.

Slocum dismounted and walked slowly into camp. His legs still had a curious spongy feel to them. Never had he found a woman who could do to him what Samantha Clairmont did. It'd be a real shame having to ride off and leave her behind in Van Eyck.

The promise of more than five hundred dollars would go a long way toward easing that hurt, though.

"John! You snuck up on us." Adam Jenks looked up from the small campfire in surprise. His head swiveled to the sentry posted atop the rocks. The man looked attentive from this angle, but Slocum thought he might have fallen asleep.

"Good thing I'm on your side," Slocum said, hunkering down by the smokeless fire. He warmed his hands a spell. In the desert sundown meant heat vanished almost instantly. How it could be so burning hot in the day and freezing cold at night was something Slocum had thought on over long nights. The best he had decided was that the devil had to play somewhere and had chosen the West Texas desert.

"What word of the payroll?" Jenks asked eagerly.

"Nobody's real sure when it's due in, but the longest guess is three or four days. We're getting close," Slocum said.

"What of the guards? Has Mulholland replaced them? I don't want to break in and find that fortress closed to me."

"He's hired a couple, but they only patrol during the day. When he shuts the bank, they go home. I've been talking to the men most likely to take a job with Mulholland and have steered them out to the railroad camp to look for work."

"I heard rumors about you chasin' down this Barstow character. Truly now, John, was that a wise thing to do?"

"I couldn't let him gun down a prisoner in my very own cell and not do something." Slocum hated the idea of considering Dunphy "his" prisoner being killed in "his" jail.

"Reckon not," Jenks said. "You got to maintain the fiction of bein' a serious candidate." The outlaw moved slightly, then reached over and moved Slocum's badge so it reflected the pale firelight. "Never thought I'd see this on your chest. Hell, never thought I'd be sittin' around a fire sharin' coffee with a sheriff!"

"Is that what you call this mop water?" Slocum spat out a mouthful of the coffee into the fire. It sizzled and hissed and flared slightly. "What all did you put in it?"

"Just a little booze to keep the boys happy," Jenks said. "Not so much it'd affect their judgment none."

Slocum glanced toward the dozing sentry. The guard either needed more to pass out or less to stay awake. Slocum pushed that aside. He had important details to discuss.

"I figure I can get into the bank without needing to blow it wide open or pry off the bars. Sawing through them would take all night."

"You gonna act as sheriff to get a key?" Jenks wasn't entirely stupid. "That's good. And we got the dynamite once we get inside. We might need a drill or two and a sledgehammer and pry bar, but them's easy to come by."

Something in Jenks's words caused Slocum to prick up his ears. He wasn't hearing something he ought to, and he couldn't put his finger on what it was. The man behind Jenks had the bedroll wrapped around the dynamite. Even if it was oozing nitroglycerin, it would do for their blasting.

Slocum remembered all that had been said—and not said.

"Where are the blasting caps and fuses?"

"Blasting caps? Why do you need anything like that?" Jenks asked.

Slocum's heart sank.

"I let old Pecos do the worryin' about the dynamite. He's the one with experience."

"Is that one Pecos?" Slocum asked, pointing up to the sentry. He wasn't too surprised to find that it was the sleeping guard. "Get him down here. We got to work fast if we're going to be ready. That payroll might show up tomorrow or it might be a few days. Either way, we've got to move fast and not make any mistakes."

"Pecos!" Jenks bellowed. "Get your butt down here. Slocum's got a question or two to ask." Jenks sank back down by the fire and poured himself more of the whiskey-laced coffee. "Truly, they are like children at times. You got to tell them every danged thing."

Slocum was beginning to think he'd thrown in with a bunch that didn't have a lick of sense among them. Even if Jenks or Pecos hadn't known they needed blasting caps, one of the other two should have. It wasn't as if this was sacred knowledge.

"What's up, Adam?" Pecos rubbed the sleep from his bloodshot eyes. He blinked twice when he noticed Slocum sitting next to his boss. As far as Pecos was concerned, Slocum had materialized out of thin air like some ghost.

"Go on, John, ask him."

"Do we need blasting caps and black fuse?" Slocum asked point-blank. "You showed me sticks of weeping dynamite but no caps."

"You need blasting caps?" Pecos scratched his head as if this was news to him. "We always just put it in and shot at it with our six-shooters."

Slocum knew there was no reason to get upset. If he had any sense he'd simply get on his horse and ride off. Better to be poor than dead or caught by someone like Sheriff Tallant. The itch of hemp around his neck was too recent a memory to forget easily. This kind of oversight was likely to run throughout Jenks's bank robbery. Slocum heaved to his feet, trying to come to a decision about what he should do.

"You're the one doing most of the planning," Pecos pointed out. "You better tell us what all we need, 'less we get into that bank and find we're some lawman's buzzard bait."

What he said was right. Slocum was the one calling the shots. If everything looked right, *then* they'd go for the payroll. If anything looked the least bit askew, he'd ride and let Jenks and the others decide for themselves what they wanted to do. The carrot of so much money dangling in front of them would see them all through the robbery, but Slocum wanted more than the payroll.

He wanted his freedom and time to spend the take.

"We need the caps and fuse," Slocum said. And he knew where they could get them without arousing any attention. If they robbed the Van Eyck general store, the shopkeeper would certainly notice. He didn't have enough stock to cover even a small robbery. Slocum reckoned they needed at least a half dozen blasting caps, and a dozen would be even better. The mercury fulminate caps were notoriously fickle about blowing off hands as often as they refused to ignite. And the black fuse guaranteed them the chance to get away in time to keep from being pulverized along with the wall surrounding the vault.

"Mount up, Jenks. We're going to the railroad camp."

"Why?" asked Pecos. "It's a goodly ten miles from here. It'll take half the night to—"

"The caps, you fool," snapped Jenks. "To lay track they have to blast through rock. We might even get some dynamite to replace that leaky stuff you got over there." Jenks pointed to the bedroll. Slocum saw saplike residue soaking through the blanket. Working with that load might be enough to send them all to the promised land.

"Just the caps. The super might keep closer count on the sticks of dynamite. We want to sneak in, grab what we need, and leave without letting anybody know we were even there."

"How many of us should go on this foray, John? Truly, I don't think we ought to leave this camp just yet. It is a good base, near Van Eyck, almost—"

"Pecos comes with us, since he's your expert." Slocum didn't try to keep the sarcasm out of his words. "You ought to come, too, just in case. Let Johnny and Ed catch up on their sleep." Slocum saw that they were already curled up on their bedrolls sawing wood.

They rode in silence, Slocum pushing the pace. He wanted to get to the railroad camp in time to ride back to town before sunup. March was starting to sling mud, and Slocum didn't want to explain what kept him away all night. Chasing down an outlaw wasn't a good answer because that only led into a passel of more lies. Sooner or later Slocum would trip himself up and March might end up throwing him in the calaboose.

"Can we slow down a mite, Slocum?" complained Pecos. "I'm not used to ridin' this long, and it's hard going for my horse in the dark."

The moon was a waxing thin sliver that provided almost no light, but Slocum didn't even answer. He kept pushing ahead. He wanted to find the weak links now, before the robbery, before they did anything that might get them killed. Pecos wasn't too high on his list of people he wanted at his side, and Adam Jenks was slowly dropping.

"There's the camp," Jenks said, pointing off to their right. Slocum had gotten the campsite wrong. Then he corrected himself. He had been riding for the spot where the crews were laying track almost a week earlier. He should have known the railroad would have moved on. Stupidity was contagious, and he'd caught quite a dose from Pecos.

"I'll circle and scout for any sign of guards. They might not bother out here in the middle of nowhere." Slocum made sure Pecos and Jenks knew where he'd meet them, then started on his quick reconnaissance. It took more than an hour to make a superficial examination of the camp. Better than a hundred men bivouacked there, if he was any judge. A few large tents housed the foreman and super on the job. Any director of the road that came out here would stay in his posh railcar rather than a drafty tent.

But the tents held his attention. That was where the dynamite and other equipment would be stored. Slocum kept riding until he found an arroyo leading within a hundred yards of a tent that must be loaded with what they needed most. It was set away from where the railroad crew slept and had a single guard dozing in front of it.

Slocum returned and quickly outlined his plan. "We'll take only a dozen caps and twenty feet of black fuse. Be sure it's one-foot-per-minute burn." The expression on Pecos's face told Slocum the man couldn't read.

"I'll go in with you, John. Truly, this is exciting," said Jenks, covering for his henchman. Slocum appreciated loyalty but preferred to be totally honest. He let it pass this time.

"We go up the arroyo, then crawl on our bellies to the rear of the tent. Nobody's got it under surveillance from the rear. If we make a little noise, the guard'll probably think a rabbit or a rattler got inside and ignore it. But we can't make too much noise or we'll get caught."

"Sure you don't want me to take a few new sticks of dynamite?"

Slocum shook his head. Getting in and out without being caught was more important. The foreman might do an inventory and find the sticks missing, then set up a hue and cry that could reach all the way to Van Eyck. As town sheriff, Slocum didn't want to have to deal with the theft. It was more important to stay close to the bank and wait for the fat payroll to be deposited.

"Let's go," he said. Pecos stayed with the horses, working to keep them quiet. Slocum wondered what the man was good at. As far as he could tell, not much.

Another forty minutes brought Slocum and Jenks out of the arroyo and within sight of the tent. Canvas flapped in the tender night breeze, covering small sounds they might make. Slocum bit back a curse when he brushed into a prickly pear pad, but Jenks yelped when he drove a sharp stone into the palm of his hand.

Slocum and Jenks went to ground, waiting. Ten minutes passed before Slocum motioned Jenks to go on. They came to the rear canvas flap and pried it up from a tent peg. Slocum wiggled through and sat cross-legged in the dirt to find the crates he needed. It was pitch black inside and he wanted to strike a lucifer but knew he shouldn't. The hiss or the smell of sulphur would alert the sleeping guard.

"Here, John, truly I think this is what we need!"

He made his way to Jenks's side and peered at the lettering on the sides of the crates. They'd found a half dozen cases of blasting caps, a roll of black miner's fuse, and even a case of dynamite. Slocum wondered where the rest was stored. This single crate wasn't enough to blast more than a few tons of rock.

"Hurry up," Slocum said. "Stuff the caps into your pocket. I'll get the fuse and—"

He froze when he heard the crunch of boots outside on the desert sand. The flap pulled back and a deep voice boomed, "I'll get it for you, Seth. Won't take a minute."

Slocum saw the man coming into the tent and another standing outside. The guard had to have been awakened.

They were caught.

14

Slocum's hand flashed for his holstered Colt, though it might be suicide to fire it within the confines of the storage tent. A single spark flying into a case of blasting caps would send them all sky high, but what choice did he have?

Adam Jenks stifled an angry response just as Slocum saw divine deliverance come arching down out of the sky.

"Fire arrows!" the guard coming into the tent yelled. "Get the hell away from the dynamite!" He let the flap close. Slocum didn't think he'd seen either of the intruders.

"What is going on?" Jenks asked, scrambling to the door and peering out the flap. "The sky's on fire with arrows. Indians!"

Slocum wasn't so sure anymore. He had spent the last ten days knocking around the countryside and hadn't seen any trace of Lipan Apaches. They might be working to hide their trail, but he knew they'd slip up somewhere. Dragging brush behind a pony covers the tracks; it doesn't do anything for manure dropped. Twigs break off mesquite trees and can't be hidden. A dozen other small traces would have betrayed the presence of Indians if they'd been out there.

"Get out the back," Slocum ordered. He scooped up a handful of fresh dynamite and stuffed it down the front of his shirt. By the time the railroad camp was finished, there wouldn't be a storage tent left standing. Even as the thought crossed his mind, an explosion staggered him back

121

into Jenks. They went down in a pile, scrambling to regain their balance.

"Move," Slocum said. "I'm going to torch this place to cover our tracks."

"Truly now, there's something I didn't want to see," muttered Jenks. Slocum looked at the top of the tent. An arrow had cut through the thick canvas. Fire spread slowly at first, but all too quickly Slocum got a good look at the night sky. More flaming arrows arched above, landing in the camp and sowing confusion. Most of the railroad track-men were dog-tired from their strenuous work all day. To be awakened this abruptly by such danger panicked many of them who wouldn't have batted an eye if it had happened at high noon.

Slocum jerked back the bottom flap and was covered with a shower of sparks from the burning canvas. He hit the ground hard and rolled, trying to put the embers out that had ignited his shirt. Rolling over and over on the sticks of dynamite hurt, but not as much as if the dynamite exploded. It took shock to detonate the dynamite, but Slocum didn't want to find out a few of the sticks had leaked nitroglycerin.

"I declare, I've never seen such a sight," Jenks said, standing in the bottom of the arroyo and staring back up at the camp. Half-dressed men ran wildly through the night, contributing to the confusion. By the time the foreman got control, a second supply tent had exploded in a fiery cascade that lit the night.

"It's the Fourth of July come early," Slocum said. He didn't stop to see if Jenks was following. The other man had the dangerous blasting caps. Slocum struggled with the roll of miner's fuse and the half dozen sticks he had shoved into his shirt.

"Who's that?" came Pecos's fearful voice. "That you, Adam?"

Slocum considered putting a bullet through the man's mouth. The last thing they needed was some railroad worker out wandering aimlessly to overhear Pecos naming names.

"Ride," Slocum said. "We got to get out of here fast. They're getting organized and when they do, they'll make a sweep of the area to see if they've lost any men." He didn't want to be within a mile of the place when the railroad workers started the hunt. And with any luck he could be back in town to change his shirt before the foreman took it into his head to report this to Van Eyck's sheriff.

"Injuns, it was Injuns," Pecos said, more than a little fear in his voice. "I saw them firing those arrows. God, it was horrible!"

Slocum rode closer to the panicked man and asked, "Did you actually see an Indian or just the flaming arrows?"

"I seen 'em. Must have been a dozen. A hundred or more! It was awful!"

Slocum dismissed anything else Pecos might say as balderdash. The man was afraid and invented bogeymen to justify his cowardice. Slocum hadn't had much chance to watch, but one person might have fired all the arrows. It would have been a feat of incredible skill, but it was possible. And it had pulled his bacon out of the fire again.

They returned to Jenks's camp, Johnny and Ed jumping up and demanding to know what the explosions were. Slocum was surprised that the detonations had been heard so far away. Every stick of dynamite in the camp must have gone up—except the six sticks Slocum had rescued at the last minute.

"Take this and keep it safe," he told Pecos, handing over the dynamite. "And Jenks has the blasting caps." He dropped the roll of black fuse and watched it unsnake slowly. Too much was happening that he didn't have a handle on. He wanted the payroll robbery to be over and have those greenbacks riding in his saddlebags.

He left Jenks and the others without another word. He had a long ride back to town and wanted to get there before sunup. Too many people would ask about his soot-blackened face, his burned shirt, and where he had been.

Slocum ached from the nightlong ride and the brush with getting burned alive and blown sky high. He stretched in the galvanized tub and sloshed water over the edge. He was clean enough and had washed away most of the burnt odor that clung to him. A few quick dips got his clothes washed, though he had to scrounge through his saddlebags for his other shirt. The one he had worn was too burned to wear.

On impulse, Slocum heaved out of the tub and quickly toweled off. He climbed into his spare duds, noting that the shirt was a tad small and stretched across his shoulders. It would have to do until he could get another shirt. He strapped on his cross-draw holster and hurried outside. The sun was just poking above the far horizon, promising another searing hot Texas day. He stopped across the street from the bank and waited to see how the morning guard duty was set up.

And he kept an eye on Mrs. Parman's Boardinghouse. Before the sun had eased another fraction of an inch in the east, Slocum heard the pounding of a horse's hooves. Whoever the rider was went around to the rear of the boardinghouse. He looked around and saw the citizens of Van Eyck beginning to stir.

He walked quickly to the side of the bank so he could see behind the boardinghouse, but the rider was gone. Slocum felt a curious elation mixed with a hollowness. He still didn't know what was going on, but one thing was certain. He was being lied to.

"Sheriff Slocum, what are you doing out here?" demanded the portly banker. Mulholland rolled along the boardwalk, the wood creaking under his weight.

"Just a hunch, Mr. Mulholland. Didn't figure you'd mind if I stood watch outside the bank for a spell."

"You been here all night?" The banker's eyebrows arched up into incredulous wigglyworms. No one did him any favors.

"Most all," Slocum lied. "Reckon I was spooked over nothing. There wasn't even a fight nearby."

"What do you mean? I heard tell of a regular donnybrook at that miserable hole of Fenneman's."

"Near the bank's what I meant. The fight was down yonder." Slocum motioned vaguely.

"Good, glad to hear it." Mulholland stopped and stared at Slocum for a moment, as if weighing his character and finding him wanting. It wasn't much of a secret that March's campaign money came from the banker, but why Mulholland wanted that reprobate as sheriff was beyond Slocum. There were too many ins and outs of politics for him to appreciate.

"Better make my morning patrol," Slocum said, as if he did this every morning. He seldom got up this early when he was in a town.

"A moment, sir," Mulholland called after him. "If you will come by the bank around ten o'clock I would like to have a conference with you."

"Might be tied up then," Slocum said, wondering what was on Mulholland's mind.

"There will be others here. Important others. Be there." The stout banker stomped off for his bank. Slocum watched as he fumbled through a key ring and unfastened three locks. Then Slocum went off whistling a cheery song. This day was turning into a good one.

Slocum found himself a good café at the edge of town and got the biggest breakfast on the menu. He still had money left from Dunphy's take of the stage robbery. He could afford the six dollars for the thick steak and potatoes, washed down with enough black coffee to float the entire town of Van Eyck. As he ate he stared out the small front window, thinking hard about the robbery. He had most of the broad plan well in hand. The details ought to take care of themselves.

What kept cropping up as a complete mystery were the Apaches and their fire arrows. Twice he had been rescued, and twice he had the feeling that Indians weren't responsible. But if the Lipan Apaches weren't pulling the bowstrings, who was? And why did they keep saving him? He would have been in more than hot water if he'd been caught by the railroad guard. More than hot water. He'd have been shot on the spot and sent straight to hell.

Somebody was watching out for him, and that bothered him most of all. He didn't want his plans or whereabouts known that precisely by anyone. He kept moving so Jenks couldn't—quite—get to him. If Jenks tried to double-cross him like Barstow had, he wanted to be able to slip free.

The thought of Barstow still running loose turned Slocum cold inside. He'd have to concentrate more on the outlaw when he finished robbing the bank. He checked his watch and saw that he had almost an hour before the meeting with Mulholland. Whatever that was about, Slocum thought it would be to his benefit to attend. Mulholland had hardly noticed him up till now.

Slocum considered a piece of fresh peach pie, then decided against it. His belly bulged from so much food. He had gotten used to the sparse tucker out on the trail. A can of beans or jerky could never compare to a juicy steak and fried potatoes.

Walking slowly to settle his breakfast, he went past the boardinghouse. The curtains in Samantha's room were pulled back to let in the morning light. When he had passed by not an hour ago they had been closed. She was up for the day. Slocum stood and stared at the front of the rooming house, as if expecting to see her come out. He yawned broadly and knew he had to have some rest. He returned to the sheriff's office and the small cot in the corner. Slocum curled up on it and in seconds was sound asleep.

He stirred, stretched, and sat bolt upright after what seemed only a few minutes. It was almost ten. He had slept over an hour and it hadn't taken the edge off his weariness. After the robbery, he promised himself. He could sleep then. He wanted to be alert to spend the payroll money and find Barstow.

He settled the gun belt and made sure his Navy Colt rode easy, then went down the street to the Bank of Van Eyck. Two buckboards, a carriage, and several horses stood outside. Whatever the meeting was about, it was drawing important—and rich—people.

Slocum went inside and just stood for a moment, studying the people assembled in the lobby. Several had the look of hardworking men, maybe the railroad's foreman and superintendent or a crew chief. The other three men were dressed in fine suits, the like of which Slocum hadn't seen since frequenting San Francisco's Union Club. They might be the railroad's owner and directors.

"Sheriff, glad you could take the time to come." Mulholland glanced pointedly toward the Regulator clock on the bank wall. The huge black hands pointed to just a minute past ten o'clock.

"Always happy to be of service," Slocum said. The men in the fancy suits were giving him the once-over. The foreman and the others paid little attention to him, standing in a tight knot at the far side of the lobby and whispering among themselves. If Slocum had to choose between the two factions, he knew which he'd pick.

One had money and used power like a whip. The other group was made up of men like him.

"Let's get down to cases," one man said. He was tall and almost cadaverous, with deeply sunken dark eyes. But those eyes held Slocum as surely as if he had been pinned to the wall. Here was a man used to command—and to being obeyed instantly.

Slocum nodded and wondered if they were going to sit down or stand for the entire meeting. The others made no effort to use the few chairs in the lobby, so he remained standing near the lobby door. He glanced toward the workmen. They had ceased their whispering and listened attentively.

"Mulholland's shown us the security measures inside the bank. They seem adequate. We are not so sure about the safety outside the bank."

"I'm new on the job," Slocum said, "but I've been doing a good job."

"What about this outlaw shot to death in your jail?" demanded the short, middle-aged man next to the walking corpse. "That killer is still at large, is he not?"

"A Texas Ranger was riding with me," Slocum said, stretching the truth a mite, "and neither of us could find him. Fact is, there's a posse from Fort Davis led by Sheriff Tallant, and they couldn't find the bushwhacker, either."

"I do believe the Rangers' reputation is overstated," the man said. "However, it does seem Slocum was in good company. We've had dealings with Sheriff Tallant. He's a good man, and if he was unable to find the killer, there's a possibility the miscreant is across the Rio Grande and into Mexico by now."

"What protection can you offer this bank?" the living cadaver asked. His eyes burned with a light that made Slocum think of a hunting cat.

"Can't match the round-the-clock guards that were here, but I don't think you need it. I can get four or five deputies, if they're really needed. Fact is, there's nothing unusual in the bank requiring such protection, is there, Mr. Mulholland?"

The banker cleared his throat, glanced at the cadaver and said, "There will be a sizable payroll deposited here. Two months' pay for the rail crews will come in on—"

"Mulholland." The name came out small, quiet, but it carried the sting of reproach. "We have yet to determine if we are going to use your bank as our regional depository."

"Mr. Norwalk, this is a secure bank, inside and out. You've spoken well of the measures taken inside. Slocum can provide external guards." Mulholland was breaking out in a sweat. Slocum was joining him. It sounded as if the railroad president wanted to put *two* months payroll into another bank, maybe farther down the line.

"The town's anxious to show what it can do," Slocum said, doubting if Mayor Leroy would spring an extra two bits for a deputy, even if it meant the railroad's money flowing into town. "I can have four deputies on constant patrol around the bank as soon as you need them."

"You have these men on your staff now?" Norwalk asked.

"Can get them sworn in by this evening. Van Eyck's such a peaceful town there's not much call for a deputy, much less four." Slocum saw his words had a calming effect on the railroad president. He turned and discussed the matter with the other two, then motioned over the workers. They talked a spell longer.

"You might need the extra deputies when the full rail crews hit town and start spending their money. We've discussed damages with the saloon owner. Mr. Fenneman is an agreeable sort." Norwalk paused, then said, "The payroll will arrive late tomorrow afternoon. This will give you the remainder of Thursday to count the money and prepare. Friday afternoon the first of the crews will arrive with pay vouchers." Norwalk sniffed. "We do not expect there to be any money left in the account by Monday morning."

"We can handle such a large dispersement, Mr. Norwalk." Mulholland rubbed his hands together, as joyous as if he had just foreclosed on a widow and taken her last dime.

"I'd better get going if I'm to have the right men deputized by tomorrow afternoon," Slocum said. He wondered how Adam Jenks would feel about wearing a deputy's badge. He and the others in the small outlaw gang were going to make history.

They weren't going to ride off with one month's pay, but two. Slocum was already spending the thousand dollars—more—he expected to find in the vault.

15

The back of Slocum's neck crawled. Someone was watching him. He reined back slightly and tried not to look too anxious. He dismounted and pulled up his gelding's front hoof and pretended to examine the shoe. He'd just had the horse shod a few weeks back. It wasn't likely to need a new set of shoes for another couple weeks. If luck rode at his shoulder, he could afford a set of fancy Mexican shoes dipped in silver for the animal.

Slocum made a big show of working at a stone while looking behind him. The trail stretched across the desert, leading away from the town of Van Eyck and was as desolate as any other stretch he'd crossed. He dropped the foot and went around the horse, patting it and keeping a sharp eye out for any sign of movement. Whoever was tracking him was doing a damned good job—if anyone really was.

"Am I just getting nervous about the robbery?" he asked as he patted the horse's neck. A huge brown eye turned his way and blinked. This was all the answer he was likely to get from the horse. He made a final circuit, listening hard, sniffing the air, looking for the flash of sunlight off metal. Nothing. His sixth sense told him there was somebody near, though.

Slocum mounted and abruptly cut off the trail. He circled, going out a mile or more and coming back to the road. The entire way he looked for signs of other riders. There was nothing. When he turned to his original stopping spot on the road, he decided he was getting spooked by the notion of so much railroad money being stashed in Mulholland's bank. Robbing that much was nice, but robbing a man like Mulholland added spice to the theft. He had nothing against the hardworking crews on the railroad, but they wouldn't be out any money. If it was stolen before they got it, their employers would have to pony up another payroll.

It might not be deposited in Mulholland's bank, or any Texas bank, but they'd be paid. Slocum didn't think the well-dressed railroad officers would like it, but they could certainly afford it. To them, losing a couple months' pay amounted to little more than an entry in some corporate set of books. They'd howl like a stepped-on dog, but they wouldn't want their crews to stop work. Completion of a road meant everything. Without the tracks, no trains steamed along. Without the powerful locomotives, there wasn't freight. And without freight, revenues were zero.

The railroad workers would get their money.

And Slocum would be immensely richer than he was now. The notion of a thousand dollars riding in his saddlebags appealed to him. That was a powerful lot of money.

Slocum reined back suddenly and spun in the saddle, studying the trail behind him. Again he'd had the sense of being watched, and again he saw no one.

He settled down and kept riding, taking a roundabout path to Jenks's camp. Slocum didn't put much store in Pecos and the others being able to see anything smaller than a troop of U.S. Cavalry riding down on them. If he was being followed, his tracker was more than good.

Just before going into the camp, Slocum dismounted and sat, eyes restlessly scanning the horizon. He finally gave up. It didn't much matter if anyone found Jenks's camp now. The money came into the Bank of Van Eyck tomorrow afternoon and tomorrow night they'd make their unauthorized withdrawal. If anyone had trailed him, knowing where Jenks's camp was wouldn't mean a thing. They'd all be scattering to the four winds, thinking on different ways of spending their greenbacks.

He rode into camp, and again the sentry didn't see him. Pecos and Jenks sat near the fire, talking earnestly. They looked up in surprise when Slocum neared. He had the feeling of catching small children with their hands in the cookie jar.

"Didn't expect to see you this soon, John. Truly, this must be good news you're bringing us." Adam Jenks rose, as if shielding something from Slocum. Pecos rubbed out the map they'd drawn in the sand.

"Things are beginning to happen, as we'd planned," Slocum said. He tied his horse to a mesquite. There wasn't any grass nearby to graze on, but he didn't intend spending much time with Jenks. The uneasiness of having someone sneaking up came to him ever stronger.

"The payroll?" Jenks rubbed his hands together just as Mulholland had at the mention of the railroad's money.

"Tomorrow afternoon. The banker gets to count it and get ready for handing it out starting Friday afternoon. Reckon all the crews will be through town by sundown Saturday."

"Then there's not going to be a plugged nickel left in the bank on Saturday night?"

"Don't see why there ought to be," Slocum said. "Norwalk didn't say anything about supply money being put in the bank—"

"Alfred Norwalk?" Jenks's eyes widened. "He's the owner of the railroad. You talked to him?"

"Personally." This seemed to impress the outlaw all out of proportion. Slocum wondered anew about Adam Jenks. It didn't pay to be too awed by the men you were robbing. A little caution was fine, but to be successful required the firm conviction that you were smarter than the men with the money.

"What's he like?"

"Puts his trousers on just like you and me," Slocum said, irritated at the way Jenks was sniffing up the wrong tree. "He didn't say anything about money for supplies, but there's going to be two months' payroll in the bank. Those men haven't been paid in a long time."

"I see," Jenks said. He didn't sound surprised. Slocum wondered if Jenks had known and hadn't bothered telling him. And what else might have slipped his mind? Slocum shifted a little to see if anything remained of the map Pecos had drawn in the sand. It was completely obliterated.

"We've got to hit the bank tomorrow night before the payout starts Friday. We might wait until Friday morning, but there'd be others around. Thursday night is best since it gives us several hours to work."

"We can hit them as they're bringing in the money," Jenks said unexpectedly. "We don't have to squeeze it out of the vault that way."

"Too dangerous," Slocum said. "The way we agreed to is better. No risk, and we might have two or three hours head start before anyone notices. Depends on how loud a blast we make opening the vault."

"The brick soaks up sound like bread does gravy," Jenks said.

"I told Norwalk I'd be hiring four deputies." Slocum watched Jenks's eyes widen in horror. He almost enjoyed the moment of fear mirrored in the outlaw's eyes. "I reckon you four are free for duty tomorrow night."

"You mean we'll be the ones doing the guarding?" Jenks started to laugh. He held his sides and tears ran down his cheeks. "Truly, John, this is rich. The foxes are guarding the henhouse. And I don't reckon anyone would identify us if we kept to the shadows and moved around a bunch."

"Being sheriff has its better points," Slocum allowed. "The way I see it, you can come into town at sundown and start patrolling around the bank. I've got to be seen or someone will start asking questions."

"March?"

"If I don't go out campaigning, he'll make hay of it," Slocum said. "He might also send people to find out what I'm doing. We don't want that. When the town beds down for the night, then we can get to work."

"When's that likely to be?" Jenks sounded excited now.

Slocum didn't blame him. So much money was a powerful lure.

"Midnight's too early. People are still out and about. If we wait until two, that'll give us an hour to blow the vault and a couple hours to get the hell away with the money."

"Oh, this is truly fine, truly fine," gloated Jenks. "We'll show up at sundown tomorrow to be deputized, John. I knew we could count on you."

Slocum hesitated. Something about the way Jenks spoke put him on guard. He thought of the different ways he might get double-crossed and saw nothing. He'd be on patrol with them. Slocum put it out of his mind. This was another facet of the suspicion he had of being followed. After Barstow and Dunphy, he'd gotten too sensitive for his own good.

"See you tomorrow. I got to go run my campaign for sheriff." Slocum rose. Jenks and Pecos both laughed, and that was the way Slocum left them.

The uneasiness he felt just didn't go away as he rode back toward Van Eyck.

Slocum wondered if he should report to Mulholland his success in finding deputies. He decided against it, knowing the nervous banker would insist on interviewing the men. Slocum didn't trust Pecos and the others not to blurt out how they'd been in town before, posing as the New Braunfels Bunch. Jenks had enough common sense to keep his mouth shut, but they were too close to pulling off the robbery of a lifetime to risk such an interview.

Having the men on duty would give Slocum an excuse to keep them away from Mulholland. March might demand to talk to them. Slocum wasn't sure if this would be a good thing, but he'd cross that bridge when he got to it. Let the erstwhile candidate for his job show some gumption. Slocum welcomed the idea that March would be the next sheriff of Van Eyck.

"John! There you are!" Samantha Clairmont came running over, almost breathless. He paused and sniffed deeply of her distinctive perfume. This time it was mixed with an odor he knew well: horses. She had been out riding.

"What's wrong?" he asked. Her tone indicated something disastrous.

"The rumors. Haven't you heard them? Everyone's simply *buzzing*."

"Can't say I have. I don't give much credence to what everybody knows. It's usually wrong." Slocum watched as the flush slowly faded. She had run hard to catch him. He saw how her dress had distinctive creases in it from a long ride.

"The bank! It's going to be robbed!" Her blue eyes were wide and she looked horrified at the mere idea that anyone might consider such a crime.

"Who? The New Braunfels Bunch?"

"No, someone else," she said. "This is a serious matter. Are you taking steps to prevent it?"

She looped her arm through his and guided him away from Fenneman's saloon. He had ridden long and hard and had developed quite a thirst. From the way her strong hands held him, though, she wasn't going to let him drink his fill until he had convinced her a robbery wasn't in the cards.

He hoped he was a good enough liar.

"I got four men coming in to act as special deputies," he told her. "That ought to scare off any but the most determined. And even if they do get past my deputies and me, Mulholland's bank is a fortress. You've seen the inside. Steel plates and what-all."

"I'm worried about the shooting," she said. "And March insists there is going to be a robbery."

"Then why isn't March doing something about it? Talk's cheap. I'm coming around to thinking March is nothing but a blowhard who might be better off cooling his heels in jail for a spell."

"No, no, John, you can't do that. It would play into his hands. If there was any trouble, he'd say you put him in a cell to keep him from stopping it." Samantha didn't loosen her grip as she steered him down the street toward the bank. It was as if she wanted him to personally show her a robbery wasn't going to happen.

"Reckon you got a point. Him staying out and not doing anything but yelling makes him look like a fool."

"You're positive there isn't going to be an attempt on the bank?"

"Can't say that. The country's alive with desperados. Ranger Ralston's off chasing some Mexican cattle thieves. That sheriff from up in Fort Davis is hunting for stagecoach robbers. Who's to say what might happen?"

"You did chase off the New Braunfals Bunch," she said. Samantha looked up at him, her blue eyes dancing. "And you did it singlehandedly. You can take care of any old gang of bank robbers."

"The bank's safe," Slocum insisted. He hoped he didn't break out laughing. What he really meant was that the bank was safe from any robber not in Adam Jenks's gang. He had put up with being a hick town sheriff long enough. The job didn't suit him, but the money coming into the bank tomorrow at noon certainly did.

A thousand dollars for an hour's work getting through the vault with dynamite. If he wanted to call it ten days since he'd come to town, that still meant a hundred dollars a day. Being sheriff hardly paid fifty dollars a month. He worked out the sum in his head. He'd have to put in his time as sheriff for almost two years to equal his cut from the robbery. And Norwalk hadn't mentioned the supply money, but it might be there. Slocum could equal three years' salary as Van Eyck's sheriff in a few minutes.

"Why are you all of a sudden believing anything March says?" Slocum asked.

"It's not just him. A lot of others are saying it, too. Maybe they're secretly hoping it is so." She looked at the ground as she walked along, as if sharing a guilty secret. "Everyone knows the railroad passing us by means the end of Van Eyck. There's not enough money going to be coming here after the track is laid. Some other town will get all the commerce, develop as a center for the country, end up turning this into a ghost town." She indicated the dusty main street. "It's nice here. I like it."

Slocum wasn't sure why he asked, but he did. "You lived here long?"

"Most of my life," she said. "Oh, look there goes Mrs. Parman. She is leaving."

Slocum saw the older woman driving off in a buggy.

"Where she goes is beyond me. She leaves about this time every day and doesn't come in until sundown."

"Maybe she has a boyfriend nearby," Slocum suggested. Samantha laughed at the notion. "What's so funny?" he pressed. "She might have several. She's not a bad looking woman."

"You think so?" Samantha asked. "She more your type than I am?" She spun around, her skirts lifting off the ground. Slocum caught sight of white breasts bulging out from the sudden turn.

"Depends on what she wears under her skirts. I'm growing real partial to what you—don't—wear."

"How do you know that's what I'm not wearing now?" Samantha teased.

"Could always arrest you and search you to find out."

"Why bother arresting me? Just find out." Her sinewy hand almost dragged him up the back steps of the boardinghouse. Just inside the door, she raised her skirts to knee level. "Go on, look," she said.

Slocum looked around to see if anyone watched their antics. It wouldn't do if anything got back to March, or worse, to banker Mulholland. Slocum was too close to getting rich to do anything to jeopardize it. He could imagine the banker getting nervous about the temporary sheriff and actually digging into his tightly closed purse to hire extra guards at the bank.

"Well, John? What do you think?" Samantha had hiked her skirt up to mid-thigh. A hot breeze blew past and whipped the hem even higher. Slocum saw the soft blond triangle nestled between the woman's thighs and felt himself responding. He ought to be patrolling the streets, making his presence known.

He cursed himself for a fool as he mounted the back steps.

Samantha danced back to the far side of the porch. "Not here, not where everybody can see us," she taunted. Anyone who wasn't blind had already gotten a delightful eyeful. "Come on over here."

She swirled and spun and exposed herself in a series of quick turns that took her to the middle of an empty storage room just off the porch. Slocum hurried after her, not wanting to be seen, and needing the blond woman more than ever. He dropped his gun belt as he went to her, catching her in his arms and pulling her tight. They kissed and the world exploded around Slocum. He was the one spinning and swirling.

The turns took him by surprise but he didn't stop kissing Samantha. She was swinging him around and around until he finally lost his balance and fell to his knees with a hollow ring. The floor under him sagged perilously, but the woman didn't give him any time to think about it. She dropped down in front of him and wrapped her arms around his neck.

As Samantha lay back, she pulled him down on top of her.

"You know what to do, John. Do it. Now, please, I need it, I do!"

He fumbled for a moment at his fly, then released his throbbing manhood. Trapped in his trousers it had grown hard and painful. Slocum slid forward, the tip touching the woman's lust-dampened lips. Samantha leaned back fully on the floor and arched off the flooring just enough for him to slide easily into her.

Slocum gasped at the sudden warmth surrounding him, the strong muscles clutching him, the sheer desire boiling out of the woman under him. He supported himself on his hands and looked down into her face. Passion racked it, turning Samantha into something animallike. She tossed her head from side to side, the blond hair whipping around on the floor.

Something bothered Slocum, but he couldn't stop to worry. Why wasn't her hair getting dirty, the way it slid all over the floor? The floor was clean. Her hips rose and ground into his groin. She teased and tormented him with her inner muscles. A storage room floor clean enough to eat off and nothing stored here. Her long legs wrapping around his waist and pulling him deeper. Insistent motion, grinding, circular grinding pulling him in and in and in.

"John, don't stop, don't do that to me," Samantha moaned.

Slocum began moving in the way both desired most. He pulled back against the strength of her legs, then let that strength drive him back forward repeatedly. Each time a new shudder passed through Samantha, and each time Slocum wondered how long he could keep his control. He was acting like a young buck with his first woman. Samantha was gorgeous and she knew all the right things to do. Slocum wanted to keep going forever, but the mounting heat inside him put that to the lie.

He fell into a constant rhythm for a while and then surrendered to the inevitable. Samantha clung fiercely to him, holding him close, keeping him from leaving—as if he wanted to. He fought the burning tide rising within and then it was too late. The powerful release made him gasp.

He kept moving for some time until there was no reason to keep on. Samantha let out a content sigh and held him close, not letting him go. Slocum hadn't realized how tired he was. With the woman's perfume in his nostrils, he fell asleep on her breast.

16

A hand on Slocum's shoulder brought him instantly awake. He swung around fast, groping for his Colt, but it wasn't where he had thought. His heart skipped a beat, and he knew failing to find his pistol might mean death.

"John, relax. It's only me, Samantha." She put her rough hands on either side of his face and turned him around so he could see her. "Don't go on so."

"What's wrong?" he asked, sitting up. He remembered then how he had fallen asleep. Looking around the neat storage room, Slocum saw his six-shooter on the other side, near the door where he had dropped it when he had come after Samantha.

"I've just heard from a friend in my group that there's a really violent man just come to town. He's boasting how he killed your prisoner and how he's going to shoot the sheriff. He doesn't seem to know you by name but—"

"Barstow!"

Slocum dived for his gun belt and fumbled it around him, even as he was fastening his trousers and getting completely dressed. He didn't dare let the outlaw run loose in Van Eyck too long. The entire bank robbery might come undone— and Slocum wanted Barstow's hide so bad he could taste the revenge.

"John, wait. Don't go running off like this. You might be killed. Get those deputies you were telling me about to help you."

Slocum shook his head to clear the cobwebs. He couldn't remember what day it was. Then it came to him. This was Thursday and the railroad payroll was due in after noon. Adam Jenks and his men wouldn't arrive until sundown, but he couldn't get them involved without doing a heap of explaining. Besides, Barstow was all his.

"I'm sheriff," he said, hating the way it sounded so hypocritical, "and I've got a duty to do. I *want* him, Samantha."

"Wait." This time she didn't argue with him. The lovely blond came over and stood on tiptoe to kiss him firmly on the lips. "I won't tell you to be careful. That's not in you."

"I'm always cautious," he told her. "But sometimes the safest course is to take the bull by the horns." Already Slocum was going over in his mind how he would take Barstow. Some men might shoot the double-crossing son of a bitch in the back and feel good about it. Slocum wanted more than to plant him in the potter's field. He wanted to see Barstow's face as he died.

He wanted to see Barstow's face when the outlaw realized he was facing not only Van Eyck's sheriff but the man he had betrayed.

He made sure his Colt moved easily in the cross-draw holster, then checked the load. He needed all six cylinders if this became a long gunfight. Slocum wanted to stop at the sheriff's office and get another loaded cylinder, but he felt the pressure of time building on him. The sooner he stopped Barstow, the safer he was, and the more likely the bank robbery would go without a hitch.

Samantha hadn't said where Barstow was, but Slocum had a good idea. The only place a man could shoot off his mouth and have anyone listen in this town was likely to be Fenneman's saloon. He walked up to the front, squinting in the sun. He wondered how long he had been asleep on the floor of Mrs. Parman's storage room. Samantha had worn him out, but the exhaustion had run deeper than he imagined. It seemed that he was living the good life one piece at a time.

He might have a good meal or a decent night's sleep, but never in the same day.

Today was going to be an exception. He was going to take care of Barstow *and* remove every nickel in Mulholland's vault.

Slocum stopped in the middle of the street, hand going up to pull down the brim of his hat to shield his eyes. This wasn't the place to call out Barstow. He didn't want to go inside the bar, either. Men doing nothing more than having a drink and minding their own business might catch some flying lead.

Slocum stopped thinking like a sheriff and started thinking like a man who wanted to stay alive. He walked to the door of the saloon and paused a few seconds to let his eyes adjust to the dimmer light inside. It wouldn't do to walk in blind and catch a few rounds in the gut. When he was able to see, he spun in, hand dragging out his Navy Colt.

Fenneman stood behind the bar. His eyes widened in astonishment at Slocum's entrance. Others in the bar looked over and saw his drawn six-shooter. The din of conversation died.

"There something I can do for you, Slocum?" the saloon owner asked. "Don't have any more of the special bottle, but I fixed up more tarantula juice. You're welcome to some, if'n you put away that hogleg of yours."

"Where is he?" Slocum's sharp eyes darted around the large room. He didn't see Barstow anywhere.

"You mean that mangy cayuse what's braggin' about shooting you?" Fenneman laughed. "He didn't mean nothing by it. He'd put away too much and was letting the liquor talk for him."

"A couple inches shorter than me, muddy brown eyes, a wart on his cheek and a pink scar just under it. Was that him?" Slocum demanded.

"You know him." Fenneman swallowed hard, his Adam's apple bobbing furiously. "He seemed harmless enough, just like a hundred other cowboys. You mean he—"

"Where'd he go?"

"Don't rightly know. He took out of here well nigh a half hour back."

"He's over at the stables, Sheriff," came a quavering voice from the back of the saloon. "Heard him say something about findin' a new horse. His old nag pulled up lame."

"Did he flash a big wad of bills?" Slocum asked Fenneman. The saloon owner shook his head. Slocum checked the room one last time to be sure Barstow wasn't there, holding a gun on them to keep everyone quiet. Still, he backed out and stood with his back to the rough-hewn wall, thinking hard.

Barstow was more likely to steal a horse than buy one, even if he had all the stage robbery money on him. He was a mean cuss and crookeder than a dog's hind leg. If the truth would do, Barstow would still tell a whopping big lie.

Slocum had no better notion where the robber might have gone than the stable. He headed over there, watching shadows and crossing streets with a mind to his back. Several times he stopped and waited, keyed up and waiting for a gunshot that might end his life. He knew the lead would rip through him before he ever heard the bullet; it was always that way, but being alert might keep him alive a while longer.

He heard the argument inside the livery before he rounded the corner of the building. He cocked his Colt and edged closer to the open door, listening intently.

"You highway robber!" Barstow shouted. "This horse ain't worth the time it'd take to whip her all the way to the glue factory."

"Fifty dollars," came the stable owner's calm voice. He was used to just about every bartering technique and thought Barstow was trying to get a better price.

"I'll give you fifty grains—of lead!"

Slocum swung around, searching for the outlaw. The explosion inside the confines of the stable almost deafened him. The few horses in stalls along the far side went wild with fear, rearing and lashing out with their hooves. Slocum homed in on the source of the commotion. Barstow stood over the body of a middle-aged man, his pistol still smoking.

Slocum knew better than to give any warning. He didn't want a shootout. He wanted Barstow dead. But the outlaw glanced over his shoulder and blurted, "Damnation!" He fired twice, driving Slocum to cover.

Slocum returned fire, but he didn't hit Barstow. He wiggled on his belly toward a stall and got his feet under him.

"That you, Slocum? I thought Tallant musta strung you up by now."

Slocum didn't respond. He had nothing to say to Barstow. He wanted the man dead. Waiting was a talent he had honed during the war, sitting on a lonely hill and waiting for the flash of sunlight off a Yankee officer's braid. Slocum had sat for days and never fired a shot and had once let an entire regiment pass him by rather than take a bad shot.

Barstow's patience wore thin, just as Slocum knew it would.

"You turnin' coward on me, Slocum? Come on out and let's do this right. Just you and me."

Barstow moved and so did Slocum. He rose above a stall, aimed, and fired. Barstow's hat went flying, but his head wasn't in it. Slocum didn't know how much he'd missed the outlaw, but it was too much. He might not have even drawn first blood.

"You got me, Slocum, you done kilt me!"

Slocum didn't fall for the trick. He crouched down and left the stable, working his way around to the rear. He wanted to go through a tack room door and get the drop on Barstow from the outlaw's rear. He almost collided with Barstow as he was leaving through that very same door.

Shots were exchanged and Slocum dove for cover behind a watering trough. He tried to follow Barstow, but the wily bandit got away from him. Slocum checked his six-shooter to be sure of the rounds remaining. He had three. Then it was two. He sighted and fired when he saw the flash of Barstow's bandanna.

This time the howl of pain he got was real. He hadn't hurt Barstow too badly, but an arm wound slowed any man down. Slocum went after his quarry, sure of the kill to come. His confidence almost cost him his life.

Barstow opened up on him, two rounds singing past his face. Slocum fell facedown in the dust, feinting to the right and rolling left. Two more rounds kicked up tiny puffs of dust where he had been. Barstow had reloaded; Slocum didn't have that luxury. He had the ammo but not the time.

"Come on, Slocum, come and eat my lead. If that misbegotten sheriff can't take care of you, I sure as hell can!"

Slocum knew the gunshots would bring curious bystanders. He couldn't let Barstow blurt out anything about them being partners in the stagecoach robbery. He had to finish the outlaw off now. Gambling his life, Slocum swung out from the corner of the building that had shielded him and looked around. A flash of sunlight on blued metal caught his eye. He fired instinctively.

His bullet ripped through Barstow's sleeve. The hot lead might have drawn blood, but it didn't slow the outlaw much. Slocum drew back his hammer for the last shot in his six-shooter and felt a grinding in the cocking mechanism. The dirt-sensitive Colt had jammed.

Barstow smiled in triumph, lifted his heavy six-shooter, and aimed, ready to kill Slocum. The shot rang out and Barstow stood for an instant, still smiling, then tottered and fell facedown in the alley.

Slocum stared dumbly at the jammed pistol in his hand. Too much rolling in the dirt had jammed the firing mechanism. Where had salvation come from?

"You're one hell of a man in a gunfight, Sheriff," came the cold words from behind him. Slocum looked over his shoulder and saw the Texas Ranger standing ten feet behind him. "I heard the shots and came to investigate. Saw the stableman dead and figured I was needed."

"That's Barstow," Slocum said, unable to think of anything else to say to Ralston. The huge ranger pushed past him and went to the fallen outlaw's body, rolling him over with the toe of his boot.

"Yep, sure is. That lawyer he killed can rest in peace now."

"Why'd you come back? For him?" Slocum worked to clear his pistol. A small pebble had lodged itself in the cocking assembly. He pried it loose and the cylinder turned freely once more. A live round—his last—lay under the hammer.

"I came looking for him, yeah, but I didn't think he'd be in town. Those Mexicans hightailed it over the border when they heard I was after them. I couldn't chase them back into Mexico without stirring up a hornet's nest of trouble with the federales. I spent a day making sure things were back to normal on this side of the river and then rode back. Just in time, from the look of it."

"Much obliged," Slocum said. "What you going to do now?"

"Get my horse watered and fed and get on back to my company," Ralston said irritably, as if Slocum was the village idiot. "Watch yourself, Sheriff." Ralston spun around and walked off, long strides carrying him to the end of the alley.

Slocum lifted his Colt and aimed it directly between the ranger's shoulders but didn't pull the trigger. The ranger was riding on and would be halfway to El Paso before hearing of the bank robbery. Slocum turned and looked at Barstow on the ground.

"You double-crossing bastard," Slocum said and fired into the man's body. It didn't twitch.

And it didn't make Slocum feel any better. He had been cheated out of his revenge. He wouldn't be cheated out of the triumph of robbing the Bank of Van Eyck.

17

"Who's going to pay for the burial?"

Slocum stared at the undertaker as if the man was speaking some foreign tongue. He looked from the mortician to Barstow's body and back, trying to make sense of it. He'd heard the words but didn't understand the problem.

"I need to know if the town's paying for his burial or if this is another one going out to the potter's field. It's getting mighty crowded there, and I don't want to start planting them standing up. The deceased didn't have more'n eight dollars in his pockets, not enough to pay for a funeral." The undertaker wrinkled his nose and sniffed delicately. "At least, not a decent one."

"He only had eight dollars on him?" He stared at Barstow again, wondering how a dead man could continue to double-cross him. Where was the money taken from the stagecoach robbery? Dunphy had fifty dollars in greenbacks stuffed into a shirt pocket and Barstow had only eight. He couldn't have spent it that fast, not being on the run and stealing horses and food as he went. Slocum reckoned at least a hundred dollars was missing, maybe more. Maybe lots more.

"That's all I found, Sheriff," the undertaker said in his sarcastic voice, hinting that Slocum might have beaten him to any money.

"I don't know how these things are handled. Can't you just prop him up next to the signpost at the edge of town and let the buzzards eat him?" Slocum almost laughed at the shock and outrage this suggestion caused.

"Certainly not, sir. Why that would pose a considerable health hazard. And it would be terribly unsightly. Decaying bodies must be buried. Soon."

"Get him into the ground before sundown," Slocum said, thinking how snakes never quite died till then. He wanted Barstow taken care of before the bank robbery. Slocum wasn't superstitious, but dead eyes might just jinx all his planning.

Slocum walked away to let the undertaker do his work. Barstow didn't deserve even this much attention. If Slocum had gunned him down out in the desert away from prying eyes, only the ants would have known his final resting place.

The sun had climbed higher into the sky than Slocum had anticipated. The gunfight hadn't lasted more than a few minutes, even if it had seemed an eternity to him. Now that Barstow was out of the way, he could focus only on the bank. His eyes narrowed as he saw the brick building. It was a fortress, and he was going to just walk right in and blow its vault open tonight. That would make up for the loss of the money from the stage robbery.

He went to Fenneman's saloon and leaned against the bar. Only a few men were drinking, and they weren't doing a good job of it. One lay sprawled across the table, as if he'd spent the night in that position. Only the loud snoring told Slocum the man was even alive. Two others sat at the far back table, shots of amber liquor in front of them, but they were more interested in a game of gin rummy.

"Heard what went on over there. You and the ranger took care of that backshooter, eh?" Fenneman scratched at his stubbled chin and then dived under the bar to find the right bottle for Slocum. It didn't quite bubble when he poured it, but Slocum knew this was potent rotgut. He sipped at it and was glad he did. It cut like a knife.

"I didn't have much to do with it. Ralston's the one who gunned him down. I owe my life to him."

"You sound bitter. The ranger's not a bad sort. A little big on himself, but they all are. Once heard two of 'em get into a bragging match. You can't believe what they claimed they'd done. Davy Crockett and Paul Bunyan rolled up together, with just a speck of Pecos Bill tossed in for spice."

"Just don't like rangers, I reckon."

"They do get in the way, even if they are just passing through," Fenneman allowed. The saloon owner stood on tiptoe and looked past Slocum into the street. A heavy wagon rattled up. Slocum turned to see what the commotion was.

From the half dozen armed men surrounding it, he knew the railroad's payroll had arrived for deposit in Mulholland's fortress bank. He downed the rest of the whiskey and asked for a second. Slocum wasn't going to go much farther with the drinking than this. He wanted a clear head when he talked with Jenks and his men later on. They had a big night ahead of them, and a long wait.

Slocum went over the timetable for the robbery in his head and decided two o'clock in the morning was about right. The law-abiding citizens of Van Eyck would be long in bed and sound asleep. The ones intent on carousing would be deep in their cups and not worth a used salt lick when it came to stopping a robbery.

"Looks to be an important shipment of something coming in," Fenneman said. "You know about this?"

"Might be the payroll everyone's been talking about for so long," Slocum said, not bothering to look around. He tasted the fiery liquor, then took enough to roll around inside his mouth, letting it tan the insides of his cheeks before he swallowed. He didn't turn until a ruckus from the door drew his attention.

"Set up a round on me. Hell," the burly man with two pistols thrust into his belt called out in a bass voice, "set up the whole danged house. We just brought in the payroll and we're gonna be rich this time tomorrow!"

"Don't care about that," Fenneman said. "You got the money now to pay for such generosity?"

"Here, old man." The railroad man tossed a double eagle on the bar. Slocum liked the way it rang on the wood, soft and melodious and completely golden.

"That the way you get paid?" he asked, pointing to the twenty dollar gold piece. "I figured Norwalk would pay you off in greenbacks."

The railroad worker spat accurately, hitting the brass cuspidor at the end of the bar dead center. "We don't take pansy-ass scrip. We want hard money. We work hard, we drink hard, and we want hard money. Right, men?" The cheer that went up allayed any doubt Slocum might have had about how they worked, drank, or got paid.

He wondered if they'd need a pack animal or two to move the payroll now. He had counted on greenbacks, which stuffed easily in saddlebags. Specie was something else. He started working out the sum in his head. He smiled when he figured they didn't need more than ten pounds of gold coin to pay the workers. That split five ways real easy.

Slocum talked with the men for a few minutes, accepting another drink in the process. The heavy wagon wasn't used because of the quantity of gold being transported; it was all they had in camp that would hold the half dozen men accompanying the payroll. Slocum couldn't figure out if these men had already been paid or if they'd just dipped a mite into the bag of coins for enough to wet their whistles while waiting for tomorrow's payday.

"So there we was, high up in Widowmaker Pass when this blizzard comes tearin' through. Froze the words on your lips, she did. And—" The burly railroad man stopped when shots sounded in the street.

"Stay here," Slocum said. He ran to the door and came to a dead stop. "Son of a bitch," he muttered under his breath. His worst fears had come true. Barstow had somehow jinxed him.

Adam Jenks and the three men riding with him had taken it into their heads to hit the bank now. Slocum recognized their horses outside the bank. The gold wouldn't be in the vault yet; it was just a bit past one o'clock in the afternoon.

The gunshots alerted more than the good citizens of Van Eyck. Slocum saw the giant Texas Ranger coming from the stable. And from the other end of town came March and a dozen of his supporters. March checked the cylinder of his six-shooter and those with him carried shotguns and rifles.

That was bad, but Slocum knew where the real trouble lay. Ralston wasn't going to let any gang of bank robbers escape from under his nose. It was only one robbery; why should it take more than one ranger to stop it?

"Throw down your guns. You're under arrest!" Ralston bellowed when Jenks poked his head out of the bank.

Jenks fired wildly. Ralston never flinched. In a smooth motion, the ranger pulled out his two six-guns and started firing with incredible accuracy, as if he was taking potshots at empty whiskey bottles sitting on a fence rail. Jenks clutched his belly and ducked back into the bank.

Slocum knew there wasn't any side door and the back door had been bricked over. A single lawman had bottled the Jenks gang up in the bank they were trying to rob. Getting them out might be hard, but they weren't going anywhere.

"We'll take over now, Ranger," shouted March. "We got a posse that can flush the owlhoots from the bank."

Slocum hoped that the ranger would lock horns with March and give Jenks a chance to escape. He wanted the double-crossing road agent for himself. He had been cheated out of gunning down Barstow. He wanted Jenks almost as much as he wanted the payroll the lout had gone after without telling him.

"Go on," the ranger said, backing off. Slocum wasn't really surprised. Ralston saw the impossibility of escape. One man with a rifle and enough ammo could keep Jenks holed up until he got too hungry to do anything other than surrender.

"You, Slocum, what are you doing hiding in the saloon? You with your drinking buddies?" March laughed at this, holding Slocum up to as much contempt as he could. The candidate for sheriff hadn't been shot at and was letting his bravery turn into foolish bravado.

Slocum edged out, keeping back from what might become a line of fire from the bank's front windows or door. "You're doing a fine job, March. Keep it up," he said. "Keep it up and you'll get your damnfool head blown off."

March laughed just as Jenks and his men opened up on them. Two of March's supporters sank to the ground, dead before they knew what was going on. Another took a slug high in the shoulder and started howling like a stuck pig. March proved himself no capable leader, diving for cover as he shouted contradictory orders.

Slocum stood amid the flight of bullets around him. Samantha Clairmont had come out of the general store and was in danger.

"Samantha, get down. They're shooting at you!" he yelled. She stood as if dazed by the notion anyone wanted to hurt her. Slocum sprinted across the boardwalk, felt the hot trail of a slug ripping along the shoulders of his too-tight shirt, stumbled, and fell facedown in the dusty street. More bullets danced around him, and again the ranger came to his aid. From the mouth of an alley across the street came a half dozen quick, well-aimed shots that drove Jenks and the other three back inside the bank.

Slocum scrambled to his feet and ran to Samantha, grabbed her around the waist, and pushed her back into the general store.

"John, you're bleeding. You've been shot. I was looking for you. After you didn't come back, I—"

A slug whined through the store's open door and blew splinters off a post beside Slocum's head. He pulled the woman down and pushed her farther back into the store.

"I'm all right," he said. "Somebody's tried to rob the payroll and got themselves bottled up." He tried to keep the bitterness out of his voice. Jenks had ruined everything. He was so crooked he had to screw on his pants, and now he was going to die for it. Slocum wanted the railroad's payroll, but he wanted to stay alive even more.

"How awful," Samantha said. Slocum caught the mocking in her tone. "Why don't you get those deputies you were going to bring in this evening? Surely, they can help out now."

"Can't reach them," Slocum said, not wanting to tell her the men trying to rob the bank in broad daylight were the men he was going to pass off as deputies. "Besides, March and his backers have the matter well in hand. Them and the ranger."

"This is serious," Samantha said.

"The robbers can't get out. March and the ranger have them bottled up good and proper."

"No, John, I mean for your election. You should be out there trying to arrest those miscreants. If you let March stay at the front, people will want to vote for him. People still remember how you let a prisoner get killed."

Slocum couldn't have cared less about the election. He was trying to find a way through the mess Jenks had caused so that he could get the payroll and keep his hide in one piece. It didn't look too promising on any front. The gold might be beyond his reach for all time. And if Jenks or any of the others was taken alive, they'd incriminate him. March would jump on anything the outlaws might say and use it to guarantee his election.

He might as well get on his horse and ride out, but the thought of the huge ranger on his trail stopped him. There might be an answer he had missed, but he didn't know what it was.

"Get to somewhere safe, Samantha," he told the lovely blond. "The boardinghouse is too dangerous. It's not more than ten yards from the bank and is likely to have a window or two shot out before this is over."

"But Mrs. Parman is there," protested Samantha.

"I'll see to getting her to safety," Slocum said. "You stay away, you hear?"

"Yes, John, I understand," she said in a small, contrite voice. But there was also the hint of mockery in her words. She laughed at a secret joke, and he couldn't figure out what it was.

He ducked back through the door, crouched low, and sized up what had happened. Two outlaws lay dead in front of the bank. In the mouth of the alley the ranger reloaded his six-shooters. If Slocum had to guess who had shot the pair down as they made their bid for freedom, it'd be Ralston. The posse with March fired wildly, their shots even knocking off pieces of red brick from high on the second story. As far as he could tell, Jenks and Pecos were the two left, and they still cowered in the bank lobby.

Slocum judged the distance to the boardinghouse and knew he'd be exposed the entire distance. Going around to where it was safer might take too long. Jenks was firing without aiming now, spraying lead in all directions as his panic grew. He was more like a cornered rat than a man now. And Pecos was hardly any better.

The bank's heavy front door exploded outward. Pecos held a stick of dynamite in his hand. A short fuse burned fiercely. He cocked his arm back to throw it at the knot of March's men near the saloon. Ralston's slug took him square in the chest. Pecos just sat down, eyes wide and very, very dead.

"Dynamite, the whole damned bank's gonna blow up!" came the shout. March was in the lead racing away from what they thought was certain death.

Slocum saw it differently. Pecos had cut the fuse too long. At least a minute remained, possibly two. The black miner's fuse was designed to burn at exactly one foot each minute.

"Give it up," Ralston shouted to Adam Jenks inside the bank. "There's no future in this for you. I'll see that you get a fair trial."

Slocum knew the effect the promise would have. He drew his Colt and waited for Jenks to rush out. He fired when the outlaw crashed through the door, trying to reach his horse. The bullet went wide.

Ralston's didn't. The ranger fired several times, each bullet finding a target. Jenks yelped and fell, clutching his leg. The next bullet tore at his hat. The third ripped open a gash on his cheek.

Slocum got off a second shot just as Ralston fired a fourth time. Slocum didn't know if it was his bullet or the ranger's that robbed Jenks of his life. It hardly mattered. Jenks lay sprawled gracelessly under the hot Texas sun.

"The dynamite," Slocum warned. The ranger didn't seem to hear. He walked slowly over, both six-shooters aimed at Jenks, until he was sure the outlaw was dead. Only then did he seem to notice the sputtering fuse on the dynamite Pecos had tried to throw.

Ralston reached down and snuffed out the spark between thumb and forefinger. He pulled the fuse free and looked at it disdainfully. He held it out for Slocum to see.

Like everything else in the robbery, this had gone wrong. Pecos hadn't bothered to crimp the fuse to the blasting cap. Even if it had burned to the end, the fuse wouldn't have ignited the dynamite.

"Is it all over?" came a fearful voice.

"Yes, Mayor, it's all over. Me and the ranger took care of those stinking bank robbers." March pushed through the growing crowd and stood next to Ralston.

"Good, good. Where's Mr. Mulholland?" George Leroy looked around anxiously. His shadow of an assistant, Jed, was nowhere to be seen.

"Here I am, Mayor. Good news. The payroll is untouched. The robbery has failed!"

A cheer went up. Slocum and Ralston were the only two among the living not joining in.

"A vote of thanks is due for Mr. March," cried Mulholland. "He certainly saved this bank—and this town—much embarrassment."

March used this as a chance to start a campaign speech. Slocum stepped back, not wanting to hear it. A hand touched his shoulder.

"A word with you," the mayor said. They walked a few feet away for a little privacy. Most of the people were more intent on March and his new promises of security for every citizen of Van Eyck than they were on the mayor or acting sheriff.

"I think I know what you're going to say," Slocum said. "I'm pulling out of the election. Let March have the job."

"Well, yes, thank you for all you've done, Slocum. I'm sure you can see how this looks. Of course you can keep the badge until next Tuesday's election. It's not as if we're ungrateful for all you've done, but—"

"I'll be pulling out of the election." Slocum started to remove the badge from his shirt, then stopped. Jenks had double-crossed him and ruined a perfect bank robbery, but Slocum thought there might be some chance of diverting the town's attention from his part in it. He'd be sheriff until the election, and that gave him a little more power than he'd have as a mere citizen. If nothing else, he'd be able to ride out after sundown.

His only real regret was being cheated out of revenge on two double-crossing sidewinders in one day. They were dead by the ranger's hand, and Slocum didn't have a ghost of a chance at stealing the payroll now.

18

Slocum still had a few dollars crumpled in his shirt pocket. "Pennies off a deadman's eyes," he muttered as he drank Fenneman's fierce liquor. The greenbacks had come from Dunphy when Slocum had tossed him in the cell. Slocum deserved more of it. His share of the stagecoach robbery should have amounted to almost a hundred dollars, if everything Barstow had said before they set out was right. But the man was a proven liar. Maybe there hadn't been any more money.

"What's that you said, Slocum?" Fenneman jumped to the bar and sat cross-legged in front of him. "You feelin' sorry for yourself? Don't go doin' a fool thing like that. Think of me. I'm out the money to get you registered for the election."

"How much was it? I'll pay you back." Slocum fumbled in his shirt pocket for the few bills left under the pin on the sheriff's badge. If he couldn't drink it up, he might as well pay any bills he had outstanding.

"Put your damned money away. I knew what I was getting into when I paid over my money. You'd've made a good sheriff, yes, sir, you would have." Fenneman looked at him in his cockeyed way. "First time you was ever on that side of a badge, wasn't it?"

"If you know so much about me, why'd you bother?" Slocum was honestly curious. Sheriff Tallant had taken one look at him and known he wasn't a lawman. Fenneman must have done the same, and yet he had spent hard-earned money to get him on the ballot.

"Van Eyck needs something to stir it up. Town's gotten too complacent. All the people do anymore is make speeches. Getting too boring for me."

"Are you moving on?"

"Reckon so. The railroad going past us like it did means there'll be thirsty gullets to fill in some other town. Won't be the first time I pulled up stakes. What about you?"

"There's always something else happening down the road a mile or two," Slocum said, not wanting to think about what he would do now that everything had fallen apart around him. He had an empty feeling as if he had been robbed. The ranger had taken away any measure of revenge on two treacherous snakes and any chance he had of getting the payroll was long gone.

"Hey, Slocum, come on over here," yelled March as he pushed his way into the saloon. "I'll stand you to a drink to show there's no hard feelings."

"I choose who I drink with," Slocum said. He didn't harbor any feelings toward March, one way or the other. March was a loudmouth who would probably steal as much as he could from the town coffers before Van Eyck became a ghost town. But to care, there had to be something more than there was with March.

"Then come on over to the bank for a few minutes. Mulholland's holding an open house to show off the gold before he closes down for the night."

Slocum perked up and turned around. "What'd you say?"

"He wants to let the whole town know the gold's safe. He's taking a few people on a tour. He wants you there." March looked uncomfortable issuing the invitation, and Slocum knew why. Mulholland wasn't missing any bets. Slocum might have conceded Tuesday's election already, but the tides of chance flowed back and forth strongly through Van Eyck. Two weeks earlier Slocum didn't have a chance at being elected sheriff; he'd been sheriff this past week and would be for a few days longer. Mulholland wanted to stay on his good side, just in case.

"All right," Slocum said, placing his glass on the bar with exaggerated precision. "Don't mind if I do take that tour. Lead the way."

"They're just using you, Slocum," cautioned Fenneman. "Don't know how, but they are. They're a slimy bunch. They want something only you can give 'em."

"I'd like to see the inside of that vault. Just to be sure the gold's safe," he said. Hope rose once more. He might see just the right way of getting the payroll out before the bank opened tomorrow morning. If he couldn't get in using Mulholland's own keys, there might be some other way that would reveal itself on this tour.

March chattered like a magpie all the way across the street. The sun was starting down in the sky. Slocum didn't bother looking at his watch. It was around six o'clock, and it wouldn't be dark for another ninety minutes. That gave him time to work, if he could figure out just the right entry point to the bank.

"Slocum, I'm glad you came," Mulholland said. Slocum saw the real reason why he had been invited. The railroad's president and his two directors stood just inside the lobby, looking concerned. The cadaverous Norwalk motioned to him. Slocum went over.

"Who is that prattling nincompoop?" Norwalk asked, indicating March.

Slocum told him. The railroad's owner sneered. "He's not got a brain in his fat head. What do you think of this bank now that the robbery attempt's over and done? Think it's worthy of our trust or should we find another bank?"

Slocum turned at the sound of hooves in the street. The Texas Ranger was riding slowly out of town, heading north toward his company's station in El Paso. Slocum wasn't sure if he was sorry to see Ralston go or not. The ranger had saved his life twice in one day, even as he had stolen some small satisfaction from him at the same time. Still, having the ranger out of town gave new life to Slocum's hopes of robbing the bank. With Jenks and his gang dead, Slocum considered keeping ten pounds of gold all for himself.

"Ralston's the man responsible for making the bank safe. Him and no one else."

"Heard that the bushwhacker who killed your prisoner's been found," Norwalk went on.

Slocum wasn't feeling up to bragging—or lying. "Ralston's doing again. He pulled my fat out of the fire."

"Don't like braggarts," the railroad owner said. "You're a modest man, but a competent one. I feel better knowing you're watching after my payroll. After we move on, come talk to my foreman about a job. We can use men like you."

Slocum nodded, wondering if he should be flattered. He doubted it. Norwalk knew how to use men. Puffing up their pride was only one way of controlling them. The promise of money was another, a good job yet another beyond that.

"So, Mulholland, show us your impregnable safe."

"This way, sir, this way." Mulholland bustled through the tight passage formed by a steel plate cut with loopholes and a desk, going back to the vault itself. Slocum got his first good look at it. He had heard of men able to crack a safe this strong. With the half dozen sticks of dynamite they'd stolen, it wouldn't have been difficult, but he hadn't the explosives or the time to drill.

The thick vault door opened. Mulholland held a coal oil lamp to light the small interior.

"As you can see, the vault is completely secure. The gold's on yonder shelf."

"Do you mind?" Slocum pushed past March and went into the vault. He wasn't sure what he was looking for but would know it when he saw it.

"Go on, Slocum, root around in the sack of coins and show everyone they're safe," urged Mulholland.

Slocum untied the leather thong from the sack and plunged his hand inside. He was met with cold, hard, gold coins. He pulled several from the bag and laid them flat on his hand. They shone with a soft yellow hue in the coal oil lamplight. He wanted to pour the rest of the bag over his outstretched hand, letting the gold filter through his fingers like sand. He held back.

"As you can plainly see, the payroll money is safe." Mulholland waited for Slocum to return the coins to the leather bag. Slocum did so reluctantly.

He looked around the confined vault and saw little way in or out. The wooden shelves creaked under the weight of stored records. Only two small bags held what Slocum took to be coins and greenbacks. If that heavy steel door closed, he'd be trapped forever. Even turning around wasn't easy. Mulholland had sacrificed room for safety.

"Everyone out now," Mulholland said. "You see how secure the Bank of Van Eyck is."

Slocum took a step and hesitated. He wasn't sure what it was that bothered him, but something did. He took another step and almost had the answer. He turned to go back into the vault when Mulholland grabbed him by the shoulder.

"Out, Slocum. Now. I'm closing the vault and locking it."

Slocum left, worrying at the vague feeling something was wrong inside the vault. He watched Mulholland slam the heavy door and spin the dual dials. Not one but two locks had to be successfully opened before getting anything from the vault.

"We'll be open for business at nine o'clock tomorrow morning, Mr. Norwalk. Your men can start withdrawing their pay then. Now, if I might have a word with you about further deposits, perhaps of the entire capital for your railroad—" Mulholland and the owner of the railroad went to Mulholland's desk. Slocum and March stood to one side and the other directors of the rail company knotted together, talking among themselves. Slocum saw that it was time to leave, and he did so without even bidding March a farewell. He owed the man nothing; he hadn't been any more than a messenger Norwalk had sent over.

Slocum returned to Fenneman's saloon, wondering if he ought to accept Norwalk's offer of a job. He didn't have any better prospects, and it might pay better than working as a hand on some ranch along the Rio Grande.

"Did you get the cook's tour?" asked Fenneman, setting up another shot of whiskey.

"As good as I'm likely to get. Norwalk offered me a job," he said, thinking out loud.

"You going to take it?"

Slocum shrugged. He might be better off heading east. Maybe he could go to Fort Worth or Dallas. He hadn't been that way in a year or more. He never failed to find a tinhorn who thought he knew the odds at poker better than anyone else. Slocum usually proved them wrong. He didn't have the biggest stake in the world, but it might be enough.

He got the glass halfway to his lips when he heard the cry, *"Fire!"* The saloon emptied in a flash, Fenneman along with the customers. A town like Van Eyck could burn to the ground in a few minutes and nobody wanted to be trapped inside.

"There, down the street. There's the fire!"

The crowd rushed off to start a bucket brigade. Water was scarce in West Texas, but for this they had plenty. Slocum held back, wondering what he was missing. He had heard something but couldn't place it. Then it came again. His eyes shot to the darkening sky. A flaming arrow arched high and landed in the building next to the one already ablaze. Slocum tried to track back the arrow's trajectory but failed. He waited for another fire arrow to come and when it didn't, he set off to help put out the fire. It was tiring, hard, hot work.

As he struggled to throw bucket after bucket of water on the fire, he wondered about the flaming arrows. Twice before they had rescued him. What did their appearance now mean? He didn't know—not exactly—but he had his suspicions.

An hour later, only embers remained of the undertaker's office, and the iron goods store next to it fared little better. Smoking piles of melted metal made it difficult pawing through the rubble.

"Slocum, a word with you." Norwalk motioned him over. "We were heading back to camp when we saw the fire. What's happened at the bank? Is the money safe?"

"Don't rightly know," Slocum said. "You'll have to ask Banker Mulholland about that."

"Come along." Norwalk gave orders and expected them to be obeyed. Slocum had been considering the job with the railroad. He decided he didn't need this kind of boss, no matter how good the pay. Still, curiosity drove him along at the moment. He followed Norwalk and the other directors of the railroad to the bank.

"Well, Mulholland? What's happened?"

"Nothing, sir, nothing at all. The fire was down the street. Didn't touch the bank. See? Not so much as a fleck of soot."

"Show me the vault. I have a bad feeling about this." Norwalk motioned for Mulholland to open the bank. Mulholland did, ushering his unexpected guests inside. The banker looked around apprehensively but the bank had been far from the blaze and hadn't been damaged at all.

"The vault. Open it. I want to see the gold again."

Mulholland silently obeyed. Slocum frowned when the banker pulled back the door. A thin haze of dust blew out. Nobody but Slocum noticed.

"You mind if I look again?" Slocum asked.

"I'll check," Mulholland said, pushing Slocum to one side. The portly banker bustled into the vault and hefted a bag, showing that it was the right weight. Relief spread over the banker's face.

"Well?" demanded Norwalk.

"Seems fine to me," Mulholland said, bouncing the bag up and down once more before returning it to the shelf. Unbidden, Slocum entered and stood in the center of the vault and knew then what had troubled him the last time.

"Out," Mulholland said to him, shoving him clear of the heavy steel door. "Out of the vault. I want to be sure the entire bank is secure for the night."

Slocum said nothing, but a small smile crept to his lips. For the first time that day, he thought luck was smiling on him.

19

Slocum left the bank and took a good look around Van Eyck. The gas streetlights were turned low as a precaution against more fires. He turned slowly, studying the buildings, remembering the people. The rickety saloon and Fenneman, the scraggly-beaded proprietor. A bit farther he saw Mrs. Parman's Boardinghouse. It would be some time before he forgot rescuing her from the two drunks—and meeting the gorgeous Samantha Clairmont.

Thoughts turned to the blond and the times they had spent together. Everything seemed so right to Slocum that he knew he couldn't possibly be wrong. The rest of the town meant nothing to him. The mayor and the undertaker and banker and all the rest could vanish from the face of the planet and he'd never notice. Samantha Clairmont was different; she was special.

Slocum went to the sheriff's office, where his gelding was tethered. He climbed into the saddle. The horse turned and looked at him as if saying, "What's going on? It's night."

"Out of here, old boy," Slocum said, patting the horse's neck. "We've got places to go and people to see."

The horse seemed inclined to doubt him. They got to the edge of town and Slocum paused. The smile returned to his lips as certainty seized him. He turned the horse's head and set off at a cruel pace.

Only when he neared the mouth of the box canyon where the posse had trapped him two weeks earlier did Slocum slow the headlong pace. During the hard ride, he had entertained doubts, but they always went away. Everything that had happened in Van Eyck had been staged. It had all occurred for one reason and one reason only. And he thought he knew what it was.

The canyon walls rose up steeply on either side of him. Slocum might be wrong, but he didn't think so. He urged his tired horse deeper into the canyon once more. This time there wasn't a lynch party riding down on him from behind. And it wouldn't have mattered if there had been. He knew the secret way out of the canyon, even if he couldn't find it to enter the back way.

Just before sundown he saw a thin column of wood smoke rising from a cooking fire. Slocum dismounted and led his horse closer.

A figure hunched over the fire, stirring the contents of a can with a mesquite twig. A bedroll had been spread out and looked as if it had been used at least one night. Slocum would have found this spot hours earlier if he had been able to come in the back way.

"Nice evening, isn't it?" Slocum said quietly. The figure at the fire jerked, hand going for a pistol.

"John!"

"Mind if I join you, Samantha? Splitting a can of beans isn't as good as having it all to yourself, but there're compensations."

"Oh?" she asked, arching one delicate eyebrow. "What might they be?"

"Good company, good conversation, someone to do what you want." He settled down beside her. She was dressed in man's clothing now, but he recognized the perfume through the sweat and horse odor.

"The first two are obvious, but the third?" She turned away a mite. He knew she was edging closer to the six-shooter she had in her bedroll. He ignored her move.

"Can't say I mind one bit. It was a better plan to rob the bank than I came up with."

"Adam Jenks was a poor choice of partner. And Pecos and the other two? Strictly amateurs. They got what they deserved." She seemed truly aggrieved at their incompetence.

Slocum's jaw tensed. He had wanted to deliver to them their just desserts. He said, "You work with the cards you're dealt."

"Not if you can stack the deck. You don't seem like the kind who'd be content with a pair of aces when he can have a royal flush." She leaned back on the bedroll, hands folded. In the flickering firelight he saw what had bothered him about her before. Those weren't the hands of a hothouse flower. Calluses and a few cuts marred their perfection, and he knew how strong they were.

"How long did it take you to tunnel under the bank? If you went through several pairs of gloves, it must have been well nigh the entire two months you were in Van Eyck."

"Oh, my, I did say I'd been there most of my life, didn't I? An oversight, but a detail most men would have overlooked."

"I was smitten by your charms; I admit it. What man wouldn't be?" Slocum sampled the beans. They were more filling than the jerky he'd been living on for the last twenty-four hours.

"I didn't make love to you just to make you look in the wrong direction," Samantha said. "I would have, if necessary, but in your case I enjoyed it. I wanted to share your bed."

"Don't remember doing it in bed too often," Slocum said.

"Ah, another failing of mine. Flaunting my secret and thinking you didn't notice. Yes, I tunneled in from the boardinghouse's storage room and spread the dirt out back, as if making a garden."

"I noticed the sag in the vault floor, too, and knew someone had been working hard. Did you have to blast through? Was that why you used the fire arrows to set the town to burning, to cover the blast?" Slocum passed over the last half of the beans. Samantha took it and ate with gusto, just as she did everything.

"Of course. It wasn't too hard replacing the planking to make it look as if the vault was intact. It never hurts to cover your tracks and confuse your enemy." She licked her lips and smiled her wicked smile. "And you know I rescued you twice before. You would have been caught in the railroad camp. You should never have gone with Jenks. He was bad luck. I'd already gotten the dynamite I needed."

"You substituted rocks for the gold in the sack."

"And cut paper for the greenbacks on the shelves. Banker Mulholland had close to six thousand dollars in his vault, in gold and scrip." She pointed to her saddlebags. Slocum reached over and undid the leather straps. Gold double eagles and wads of greenbacks stared up at him.

"Why'd you save me the first time? From the Fort Davis sheriff?"

"Maybe I knew I'd need someone to help me later, if anything went sour," Samantha said, her blue eyes glowing in the dim light. Her hair had turned to liquid silver and Slocum had never seen a more beautiful woman. And he had certainly never crossed paths with one so ambitious and daring.

"No," Slocum said. "That's not it."

"Maybe I'd crossed Tallant before and hated that man's weasely guts."

"Possible, but it still doesn't explain it."

"I liked your looks."

Slocum leaned over and kissed her on the lips, then reached under the blanket and put his hand atop hers where it rested on her six-shooter. Their eyes met and a smile danced on Samantha's lips. With her index finger, she traced around the rim of the badge he had forgotten to remove.

Slocum pulled the sheriff's badge off and tossed it into the fire.

"Fifty-fifty split?" he asked.

"Let's discuss it in the morning." Samantha smiled again

in her wicked, wanton way and her arms circled his neck, carrying him down to the bedroll. The moon rose and the fire died to coals around the molten badge and neither Samantha nor Slocum noticed.

I was hurt, though how badly I didn't know. Some three hours earlier I'd been shot, the ball taking me in the left side of the chest about midway up my rib cage. I didn't know if the slug had broken a rib or just passed between two of them as it had exited my back. I'd been in Galveston, trying to collect a gambling debt when, like a fool kid, I'd walked into a set-up that I'd ordinarily have seen coming from the top of a tree stump. I was angry that I hadn't collected the debt; I was more than angry that I'd been shot, but I was furious at myself for having been suckered in such a fashion. I figured if it ever got around that Wilson Young had been gotten that easy, all of the old enemies I'd made through the years would start coming out of the woodwork to pick over the carcass.

But, in a way, I was lucky. By rights I should have been killed outright, facing three of them as I had been and having nothing to put me on the alert. They'd had guns in their hands by the time that I realized it wasn't money I was going to get but lead.

Now I was rattling along on a train an hour out of Galveston, headed for San Antonio. It had been lucky, me catching that train just as it was pulling out. Except for that, there was an excellent chance that I would have been incarcerated in Galveston and looking at more trouble than

175

I'd been in in a long time. After the shooting I'd managed to get away from the office where the trouble had happened and made my way toward the depot. I'd been wearing a frock coat of a good quality linen when I'd sat down with Phil Sharp to discuss the money he'd owed me. Because it was a hot day I'd taken the coat off and laid it over the arm of the chair I was sitting in. When the shooting was over I'd grabbed the coat and the little valise I was carrying and ducked and dodged my way through alleyways and side streets. I'd come up from the border on the train so, of course, I didn't have a horse with me.

But I did have a change of clothes, having expected to be overnight in Galveston. In an alley I'd taken off my bloody shirt, inspected the wound in my chest, and then wrapped the shirt around me, hoping to keep the blood from showing. Then I'd put on a clean shirt that fortunately was dark and not white like the one I'd been shot in. After that I'd donned my frock coat, picked-up my valise, and made my way to the train station. I had not known if the law was looking for me or not, but I'd waited until the train was ready to pull out before I'd boarded it. I'd had a round trip ticket so there'd been no need for me to go inside the depot.

I knew I was bleeding, but I didn't know how long it would be before the blood seeped through my makeshift bandage and then through my shirt and finally showed on my coat.

All I knew was that I was hurting and hurting bad and that I was losing blood to the point where I was beginning to feel faint. It was a six hour ride to San Antonio and I was not at all sure I could last that long. Even if the blood didn't seep through enough to call it to someone's attention I might well pass out. But I didn't have many options. There were few stops between Galveston and San Antonio, it being a kind of a spur line, and what there were would be small towns that most likely wouldn't even have a doctor. I could get off in one and lay up in a hotel until I got better, but that didn't much appeal to me. I wanted to know how bad I was hurt and the only way I was going to know that was to hang on until I could get to some good medical attention in San Antone.

I was Wilson Young and, in that year of 1896, I was 32 years old. For 14 of those years, beginning when I was not quite 15, I had been a robber. I'd robbed banks, I'd robbed money shipments, I'd robbed high stakes poker games, I'd robbed rich people carrying more cash than they ought to have been, but mostly I'd robbed banks. But then, about four years passed; I'd left the owl hoot trail and set out to become a citizen that did not constantly have to be on the lookout for the law. Through the years I'd lost a lot of friends and a lot of members of what the newspapers had chosen to call my "gang," calling it the Texas Bank Robbing Gang in one headline.

I'd even lost a wife, a woman I'd taken out of a whorehouse in the very same town I was now fleeing from. But Marrianne hadn't been a whore at heart, she'd just been kind of briefly and unwillingly forced into it in much the same way I'd taken up robbing banks.

I had been making progress in my attempt to achieve a certain amount of respectability. At first I'd set up on the Mexican side of the border, making occasional forays into Texas to sort of test the waters. Then, as a few years passed and certain amounts of money found their way into the proper hands, I was slowly able to make my way around Texas. I had not been given a pardon by the governor, but emissarys of his had indicated that the state of Texas was happy to have no further trouble with Wilson Young and that the past could be forgotten so long as I did nothing to revive it.

And now had come this trouble. The right or wrong of my position would have nothing to do with it. I was still Wilson Young and if I was in a place where guns were firing and men were being shot the prevailing attitude was going to be that it was my doing.

So it wasn't only the wound that was troubling me greatly; it was also the worry of the aftermath of what had begun as a peaceful and lawful business trip. If I didn't die from my wound there was every chance that I would became

a wanted man again and there would go the new life I
had built for myself. And not only that life of peace and
legality, but also a great deal of money that I had put into
a business in Del Rio, Texas, right along the banks of the
Rio Grande. Down there, a stone's throw from Mexico, I
owned the most high class saloon and gambling emporium
and whorehouse as there was to be found in Texas. I had at
first thought to put it on the Mexican side of the river, but
the *mordida*, the bribes, that the officials would have taken
convinced me to build it in Texas where the local law was
not quite so greedy. But now, if trouble were to come from
this shooting, I'd have to be in Mexico and my business
would be in Texas. It might be only a stone's throw away
but, for me, it might just as well be a thousand miles. And
I'd sunk damn near every cent I had in the place.

My side was beginning to hurt worse with every mile. I
supposed it was my wound but the train was rattling around
and swaying back and forth like it was running on crooked
rails. I was in the last car before the caboose and, every
time we rounded a curve, the car would rock back and
forth like it was fixing to quit the tracks and take off across
the prairie. Fortunately, the train wasn't very crowded and
I had a seat to myself. I was sort of sitting in the middle
of the double cushion and leaning to my right against the
wall of the car. It seemed to make my side rest easier to
stretch it out like that. My valise was at my feet and, with a
little effort, I bent down and fumbled it open with my right
hand. Since my wound had began to stiffen up, my left arm
had become practically useless—to use it would almost put
tears in my eyes.

I had a bottle of whiskey in my valise and I fumbled
it out and pulled the cork with my teeth and then had a
hard pull. There was a spinsterish looking middle-aged lady
sitting right across the aisle from me, and she give me such
a look of disapproval that I thought for a second that she
was going to call the conductor and make a commotion.
As best I could I got the cork back in the bottle and then
hid it out of sight between my right side and the wall of
the car.

Outside, the terrain was rolling past. It was the coastal prairie of south Texas, acres and acres of flat, rolling plains that grew the best grazing grass in the state. It would stay that way until the train switched tracks and turned west for San Antonio. But that was another two hours away. My plan was to get myself fixed up in San Antone and then head out for Del Rio and the Mexican side of the border just as fast as I could. From there I'd try and find out just what sort of trouble I was in.

That was, if I lived that long.

With my right hand I pulled back the left side of my coat, lifting it gently, and looked underneath. I could see just the beginning of a stain on the dark blue shirt I'd changed to. Soon it would soak through my coat and someone would notice it. I had a handkerchief in my pocket and I got that out and slipped it inside my shirt, just under the stain. I had no way of holding it there, but so long as I kept still it would stay in place.

Of course I didn't know what was happening at my back. For all I knew the blood had already seeped through and stained my coat. That was all right so long as my back was against the seat, but it would be obvious as soon as I got up. I just had to hope there would be no interested people once I got to San Antone and tried to find a doctor.

I knew the bullet had come out my back. I knew it because I'd felt around and located the exit hole while I'd been hiding in the alley using one shirt for a bandage and the other for a sop. Of course the hole in my back was bigger than the entrance hole the bullet had made. It was always that way, especially if a bullet hits something hard like a bone and goes to tumbling or flattens out. I could have stuck my thumb in the hole in my back.

About the only good thing I could find to feel hopeful about was the angle of the shot. The bullet had gone in very near the bottom of my ribs and about six inches from my left side. But it had come out about only three or four inches from my side. That meant there was a pretty good chance that it had missed most of the vital stuff and such that a body has got inside itself. I knew it hadn't nicked my lungs because I was breathing fine. But there is a whole bunch of other stuff inside a man that a bullet ain't going to do a bit of good. I figured it had cracked a rib for sure because it hurt to breathe deep but that didn't even necessarily have to be so. It was hurting so bad anyway that I near about couldn't separate the different kinds of hurt.

It had been a man named Phil Sharp that had shot me. And a more unlikely man to give me my seventh gunshot wound I could not have imagined. I had ended my career on the owl hoot trail with my body having lived though six gunshots. That, as far as I had been concerned, had been a-plenty. By rights I should have been dead, and there had been times when I had been given up for dead. But once off the outlaw path I'd thought my days of having my blood spilt were over. Six was enough.

And then Phil Sharp had given me my seventh. As a gambler I didn't like the number, There was nothing lucky about it that I could see and I figured that anything that wasn't lucky had to be unlucky.

Part of my bad luck *was* because I was Wilson Young. Even though I'd been retired for several years I was still, strictly speaking, a wanted man. And if anybody had cause to take interest in my condition it might mean law—and law would mean trouble.

For that matter Phil Sharp and the three men he'd had with him might have thought they could shoot me without fear of a murder charge because of the very fact of my past and my uncertain position with regard to the law, both local and through the state. Hell, for all I knew some of those rewards that had been posted on my head might still be lying around waiting for someone to claim them. It hadn't been so many years past that my name and my likeness had been on wanted posters in every sheriff's office in every county in Texas.

I had gone to see Phil Sharp because he'd left my gambling house owing me better than $20,000. I didn't, as an ordinary matter, advance credit at the gaming tables but Sharp had been a good customer in the past and I knew him to be a well-to-do man. He owned a string of warehouses along the docks in Galveston which was the biggest port in Texas. The debt had been about a month old when I had decided to go and see him. When he'd left Del Rio he'd promised to wire me the money as soon as he was home but it had never come. Letters and telegrams jogging his memory had done no good so I'd decided to call on him in person. It wasn't just the twenty thousand, there was also the matter that it ain't good policy for a man running a casino and cathouse to let word get around that he's careless about money owed him. And in that respect I was still the Wilson Young it was best not to get too chancy with. Sharp knew my reputation and I did not figure to have any trouble with him. If he didn't have the twenty thousand handy I figured we could come to some sort of agreement as to how he could pay it off. I had wired him before I left Del Rio that I was planning a trip to Houston and was going to look in on him in Galveston. He'd wired back that he'd be expecting me.

I had seen him in his office in the front of one of the warehouses he owned down along the waterfront where they loaded and unloaded all the ships. He'd been behind his desk when I'd been shown in, getting up to shake hands with me. He'd been dressed like he usually was in an expensive suit with a shiny vest and a big silk tie. Sharp himself was a little round man in his 40s with a kind of baby face and a look that promised you could trust him with your virgin sister. Except I'd seen him without the suit and vest chasing one of my girls down the hall at four o'clock in the morning with a bottle of whiskey in one hand and the handle to his hoe in the other. I'd also seen him at the poker table with sweat pouring off his face as he tried to make a straight beat a full house. It hadn't then and it probably never would.

He'd acted all surprised that I hadn't gotten my money, claiming he'd mailed it to me no less than a week ago. He'd skid, "I got to apologize for the delay; but I had to use most of my ready cash on same shipments to England. Just let me step in the next room and look at my canceled checks. I'd almost swear I saw it just the other day. Endorsed by you."

Like I'd said, he looked like a man that might shoot you full of holes in a business deal, but not the sort of man who could use or would use a gun.

He'd gotten up from his desk and gone to a door at the back, just to my right. I'd taken off my coat and laid it over the arm of the chair, it being warm in the office. I'd been sitting kind of forward on the chair, feeling a little uneasy for some reason. It was that, but it was mainly the way Sharp opened the back door that probably saved my life. When you're going through a door you pull it to you and step to your left, toward the opening, so as to pass through. But Sharp pulled open the door and then stepped back. In that instant, I slid out of the chair I was sitting in and down to my knees. As I did, three men with hoods pulled over their heads came through the door with pistols in their hands. Their first volley would have killed me if I'd still been sitting in the chair. But they'd fired where I'd been and, by the time they could cock their pistols for another round, I had my revolver in my hand and was firing. They never got off another shot, all three went down under my rapid fire volley.

Then I became aware that Phil Sharp was still in the room, just by the open door. I was about to swing my revolver around on him when I saw a little gun in his hand. He fired, once, and hit me in the chest. I knew it was a low caliber gun because the blow of the slug just twitched at my side, not even knocking me off balance.

But it surprised me so that it gave time for Sharp to cut through the open door and disappear into the blackness of the warehouse. I fired one shot after him, knowing it was in vain, and then pulled the trigger on an empty chamber.

I had not brought any extra cartridges with me. In the second I stood there with an empty gun I couldn't remember why I hadn't brought any extras, but the fact was that I was standing there, wounded, with what amounted to a useless piece of iron in my fist. As quick as I could, expecting people to suddenly come bursting in the door, I got over to where the three men were laying on the floor and began to check their pistols to see if they fired the same caliber

ammunition I did. But I was out of luck. My revolver took a
.40 caliber shell, all three of the hooded men were carrying
.44 caliber pistols.

Two of the men were dead, but one of them was still
alive. I didn't have time to mess with him, but I turned
him over so he could hear me good and said, "Tell Phil
Sharp I ain't through with him. Nor your bunch either."

Then I got out of there and started making my way for
the train depot. At first the wound had bothered me hardly
at all. In fact I'd at first thought I'd just been grazed. But
then, once outside, I saw the blood spreading all over the
front of my shirt and I knew that I was indeed hit. I figured
I'd been shot by nothing heavier than a .32 caliber revolver
but a .32 can kill you just as quick as a cannon if it hits you
in the right place.